MICKY DONNELLY was born in Belfast in 1952. He studied at the University of Ulster from 1976 to 1981 where he obtained a BA and an MA in Fine Art. From 1985 to 1986 he held the Arts Council of Northern Ireland Scholarship at the British School in Rome and in 1989 he was awarded an Arts Council of Northern Ireland Major Bursary. Since 1981 he has participated in solo and group exhibitions in Ireland and internationally. In 1996 he was elected a member of Aosdána, one of the most prestigious positions in the Irish arts. He lives in County Laois.

FOR TOMÁS
BEST WISHES,

doubletime

micky donnelly

THE
BLACKSTAFF
PRESS
BELFAST

With thanks to Orla Dukes, John Flanagan, Noreen O'Hare and Jurgen Schneider for comments on the first draft; to John Brown and the Arts Council of Northern Ireland for their support; to Hilary Bell for her sound advice; and to the staff at Blackstaff Press for their encouragement.

First published in 2001 by
The Blackstaff Press Limited
Wildflower Way, Apollo Road
Belfast BT12 6TA, Northern Ireland
with the assistance of
The Arts Council of Northern Ireland

ARTS
COUNCIL
of Northern Ireland

Micky Donnelly has asserted his right under the
Copyright, Designs and Patents Act 1988
to be identified as the author of this work.

Typeset by Techniset Typesetters, Newton-le-Willows, Merseyside

Printed in Ireland by ColourBooks Limited

A CIP catalogue for this book is available from the British Library

ISBN 08564-693-7

www.blackstaffpress.com

With a condescending grin he offered his hand, hardly
bothering to sit up. I grasped it only because it provided
me with the curious sensation of Narcissus fooling
Nemesis by helping his image out of the brook.

from *Despair* by Vladimir Nabokov

nooks

Assholes. Fat bastards. Where did they go? They would be hopping now all right, mad as monkeys, their swollen faces fit to burst, their big bellies heaving in anger. I was gambling on their fat brains not thinking too straight. They would probably go into town, following the direction of my decoy taxi. I was chuffed as fuck with that little manoeuvre. A smart enough move, I thought, for a man in the nearest thing to a blind panic. The bug-eyed taxi driver almost had a heart attack when I'd jumped into his cab and screamed at him to drive. He almost had another one when, about twenty seconds later, I screamed at him to stop. I leapt out at the traffic lights, hollered at him to drive on, slammed the door, and then ran off into the rain. I'd thrown him a fiver in the heat of the moment, so he couldn't really complain – that was more than enough for a mere five-hundred-yard journey – but I wasn't so pleased now with my hasty act of generosity. My ill-gotten gains would soon disappear at this rate, but what the hell, I would see him again sometime and get some change out of him.

My own heart-rate had slowed down, back to normal, more or less, as far as I could tell. And I was getting my breath back, gradually, to a manageable puff. I was walking slowly, looking around, checking behind, just in case the two fat fucks weren't so easily wrong-footed. The exhilaration of my quick-witted escape soon dissipated, forgotten somehow, dissolved in the evening drizzle. The questions came back. What exactly had happened back there at the Flatfield? What should I do now? Where to go? How did I let things get to this pathetic mess? Why did I not do what I was supposed to do and get it over with? Why was I such a jerk? Questions followed by questions, and not an answer in sight. I stepped into a doorway for a few minutes, out of the rain, to settle my nerves and decide what to do. I pushed the wet hair back from my face and I noticed that my hands were shaking again.

I looked back along the street. It was quiet. There was no one about, nothing stirring. I told myself to relax, calm down, but it wasn't so easy. I'd just been through the worst three days of my life, with even worse to come if I wasn't careful. I'd messed things up even more back there in the bar. I was a jerk all right, a victim of my own stupidity, a prize turkey honing the blade.

I looked in the other direction. Nothing much happening there either except a few winos, in the near distance, circling around each other in the fading light. They were surrounded by discarded beer cans and blue plastic bags, brightly fluorescent against the wet rubble-strewn ground between two gable ends. They cursed each other loudly. I cursed them too. More victims. Hardly an ounce of sense between them, soaked and miserable, with a bus shelter and some tree cover only twenty feet away. They were fresh out of drink too, judging by their overheated exchanges. Not much luck for them tonight. Still, luck or no luck, they'd find a way to get more booze. They always did.

I was fortunate just to be standing there, I thought. I'd changed my mind within a second or two of giving myself up in the Flatfield and my luck had changed at the same time. I'd chickened out, like a useless piece of shit, was more like it, and I'd somehow managed to get away with it. At least I was in one piece, against all the odds. Reason enough to calm down, I said to myself. A lucky break, at last, but there was something not right about this charred little nugget of good luck. I took some deep breaths, and wiggled my hands about a bit, half-heartedly, knowing it would make no difference to the shakes. I needed a drink.

Something was itching at me. Some more mental baggage. Another question. When is good luck bad luck? It suddenly popped out of nowhere, complete and fully formed. I considered its implications for a while. I'd nothing better to do, after all, except watch the winos abuse each other. The more straightforward versions – what is good luck? and what is bad luck? – suddenly seemed banal and ordinary by comparison. I had surprised myself. It was nowhere in the region of a blinding insight or even close to a modest little realisation. In fact, it was kind of dumb, but somehow this question felt important. I was primed and ready for it. I had moved on a step. I had experienced a semi-original thought for the first time since the inimitable McNabb had made me painfully aware of my all too obvious faults, just two days ago, two very long days ago. He was right. Confused by bad connections in the lines of cause and effect, I'd lost the ability to take charge of even the most basic sequences of my life, but, for now at least, I had moved on to a better question. I'd made a start. Yes, for me and for McNabb, my forthright friend, my self-appointed spiritual mentor, this was a new beginning, just maybe, on the road to recovery.

I stepped back into the warm twilight drizzle. I had calmed down enough. My hands had almost stopped shaking. It was time to move on. I needed a drink badly, so I had to go somewhere. I passed the winos quickly, head down.

'Hey Myles,' one of them shouted, 'any odds?'

'No,' I shouted back.

'Fuck you,' he said. 'You stingy cunt.'

'Fuck you too, you wet pussy,' I said, and the rest of them barked and cackled in amusement.

Splashing and dripping water, I made my way directly towards Nooks hotel. It was close enough to warrant a visit and I reckoned it was as safe as anywhere else. I was also pretty sure that some of the Lads, my network of boozing buddies, would be there. I looked around occasionally to make sure I wasn't being followed, and kept up a brisk pace. I worked over my question with sustained vigour, robustly, rigorously repeating it over and over again, in the hope that it would somehow service its own requirement to be answered. I suddenly remembered a story I'd read years ago. By someone called Lin Yutang, as far as I could recall.

An old Chinese guy lives in a little farm with his grown-up son and a single horse. The horse runs off, disappears. The old man is upset, understandably so. The neighbours hear the news, by and by, and call round to sympathise.

'Such bad luck, terrible, terrible. Such a loss, bad luck, bad luck.'

This goes on for weeks. The old guy is starting to get fed up with all this forced sympathy when the horse returns one day, out of the blue, with two wild horses for company. The neighbours eventually hear the good news and call around in ones and twos, more reticent this time, but amazed by the circumstances.

'Such good fortune. Two new horses, such good luck.'

With all these horses around the place, the son is persuaded to do some work. So he decides to tame the newcomers, to break them in. He succeeds, after much effort, with the first wild horse, and is breaking in the second when he is badly thrown and breaks his leg instead. Again the neighbours come round, again sympathetic, with gifts and lots of medical advice and stories of horrendous injuries sustained in similar circumstances.

'Such bad luck to be injured this way, and such a

healthy, strapping young fellow.'

The young fellow is laid up for an indefinite period, and lo and behold, a war breaks out unexpectedly over disputed territory. The army is mobilised and all the young lads of a certain age are rounded up, conscripted, and obliged to fight for their extra territory far away. Of course, our boy is no use whatsoever with a big clumsy splint on his leg. Officials arrive and grill him mercilessly. They give him a good hearty thump on the leg just to make sure of his bona fides. His howls of agony seem genuine enough, so he's allowed to stay put. Away they go to their bloody war, and the farmer gets the neighbours round again.

'Such good luck. Such good fortune.'

So it goes, on and on.

Shape and form, shape and form, oriental wisdom, very reassuring. Drip, drip, drip.

The reverie ended abruptly when I clumped up the steps and pushed open the door to the foyer of Nooks, a modest kind of hotel with a boringly bland open-plan bar on the ground floor. It was owned by superstitious Chinese with a perverse sense of humour and a fear of bad feng shui. It was certainly not one of my favourite haunts, but convenient on certain occasions. The doorman-cum-bouncer, a lanky drink of water in a blue blazer – a blazer, mind you, with a little Nooks emblem sewn onto the breast pocket and gold buttons down the middle, in a Belfast pub in 1998, very reassuring indeed – stared at me with marble eyes as I shook my wet coat and wiped my boots on the emblemed mat.

'Evening,' I said, with the usual faked bonhomie, and he

had to reply, knowing fine well that humiliation received at the start of the evening was a necessary prerequisite for dishing it out at the end.

'Evening, sir.' The mumble nearly choked him, but he added the 'sir'. There was no one around to witness this exchange, this charged and unoriginal summary of our mutual disgust. But he said it anyway, because he had to, it was part of his hated job, he was told to do it. He knew that silence would have left him triumphant, but he insisted on degrading himself.

Satisfied, I passed through into the bar, shaking off water as I went. I looked quickly around. Nothing unusual so far. I stopped just inside the door to push back my dripping hair and to examine myself in the Bushmills Whiskey mirror. The reflected Myles, the only one I really knew, stared back. It was definitely a handsome face by anybody's standards, apart from the puffy eyes, emphasised by the harsh overhead light, and the small, stubborn bruise on my forehead. It would be a pity to have such a remarkable and striking countenance arbitrarily rearranged. The fact that I chickened out with the fat bastards didn't seem so bad, after all.

I turned my head slightly, just about to begin the usual scan-and-search routine, and something caught my attention. I knew immediately that my luck had indeed changed for the better. Just above the y in the whiskey, another pair of eyes, not puffy at all, were looking at mine – in a concentrated, deliberate kind of way. Then there was the mouth, red and round, moving independently of the eyes, articulating strongly, forcefully, but silent in the mirror against the mixture of music and chatter that made up the background noise. I looked back at the eyes. I held their gaze. They hesitated and then looked away, distracted by someone or something closer. The mouth still talked heatedly, maybe drunkenly, I thought, as I performed a final little optimistic flourish at the flattened hair.

I had seen her somewhere before, probably McLaverty's by the cut of her – she had long chunky silver earrings and a scruffy Scandinavian hairdo, and she wore an oddly patterned dress. Or maybe I'd come across her in one of the more trendy, arty bars recently opened in the strangest parts of the city centre, disrupting years of carefully cultivated navigation patterns. There were now far too many new bars for regular visits, but they were good for novelty value and useful for my work, when I did any work, that was. I wondered briefly when I might find the time to get back to it, but some kind of nagging survival instinct interrupted the speculation, or some conditioned reflex behaviour, I couldn't tell. Instinct or learned behaviour – I could never figure out which one had the upper hand. It was one of the many hobby-horse dualities that used to stimulate and amuse me. Myles the Dialectician had yet to become Myles the Monist, in despair, seeking that one shard of indissoluble truth behind all the double dealing. I got back to the scanning routine.

A quick turn and a careful scrutiny of the Friday night crowd revealed nothing else of much interest or alarm. Thank Christ, I thought. Maybe I could have a quiet, uneventful few hours for a change. I needed a break from chaos, just a brief interlude, and a safe place where I didn't have to deal with reality for a while. I needed to take it easy, to have a few drinks, and get my nerves settled properly. I moved towards the bar. I felt a little trickle of rainwater cruising along some path of least resistance just behind my ear as I eased and sidestepped my way through the crowd.

I was keeping a keen eye on those silver earrings as I moved. They looked Mexican, or South American maybe, sort of ethnic chic, ostentatious, a bit garish even, and probably cheap. Their owner looked good, though. Foxy, in a blondish kind of way.

She was still talking, all mouth and eyes and silver shimmy, the mouth pursing and twitching and rippling and curving in time to the pauses and rhythms of her four- or five-way conversation. The eyes, meanwhile, managed to keep up a flickering contact with their puffy counter-parts. A quaint little pas de deux it was indeed, that was to go on for most of the evening. It was hard to tell where her company started and ended in the press of people, as I pushed gradually towards a few familiar faces. Some of the Lads, penguin-like as ever in their noisy, upright shuffling manner, greeted me with their usual gruffness. I was more than glad to see them.

'All right, Myles? Hello, Myles. Hi, Myles. Want a pint?' It was always the same, the same non-committal but instantly inclusive, penguin-style greeting.

'Hello, lads. Of course.' It was always same response.

Penguin life is a wonder of nature. The constant din, the hum of bodies, the intermittent cackles and squawks, the shuffling and bumping, the ebb and flow of contact and withdrawal, and the hidden social codes are a complete mystery to the casual observer. Not so to the Lads, bless them, who stand around in bars everywhere, in groups of shifting dimensions, in changing company, in improvised rounds, or buying individually before drifting into another adjacent orbit of banter and bonding. They understand. They understand completely.

I shuffled happily into the group. They made room. I didn't have to say too much – a heavily edited account of the last couple of hours was perfectly sufficient.

'Where was I? . . . Just had a few pints in the Flatfield . . . Yeah, I saw Jonty, Marty, Soupey, and Bap. Soupey and Bap were pissed, talking shite as usual . . . No, not much biz. Jonty was saying that him and Marty went to the Tallhouse the other night for a session and bumped into Tom, Mick and Harry, who were meeting up with some girls. They all went back later with carry-outs to Harry's and ended up wrecking the place . . . Yeah, the Flatfield was busy all right . . . How come I left? There was some unwelcome company . . . Who do you think? . . . No, not the Wife. We have an arrangement now . . . Yeah, Bill and Ben, the big fat fucks, and some other pricks who were mad at me for something . . . No, they didn't get me, but there was a serious commotion, and then they all started to fight among themselves and I did a runner. I was lucky to get out in one piece. It fairly shook me up . . . Yeah, I'm all right now . . . Cheers. Fuck the begrudgers. By the way, who's yer women over there, the blonde with the earrings? . . . Is that right? . . . She drinks in the Backyard? Thought so, one of the arty crowd . . .'

The conversation settled into a rounded discussion

about the snottiness of arty girls and I had time to watch the Mexican earrings shimmer and bob and occasionally set themselves squarely in my direction. The eyes were now more cautious but they were still in regular contact, keeping tabs. She was getting drunk all right but she had at least three admirers around her, jockeying for position – competition, not much to look at, but competition. Penguin courtship. I always hated that. I began to lose interest in the mating ritual and decided to concentrate on the other, more important, penguin ritual. How many drinks were strictly necessary for the next round? Other familiar and not so familiar faces were poking into the group and it was probably better to order soon and reap the benefits later. I decided to get an early round. It had to be done, and the sooner the better.

I adopted the usual stance, the traditional posture, the only one guaranteed to ensure prompt and efficient service in a crowded Friday night bar in Belfast. I raised myself up slightly on the balls of the feet, my head tilted back at an oblique angle, eyes moving expectantly to and fro, mouth just open, ready to shout, but not too early. If I shouted too early, I might as well have gone for a swim. I had to establish eye contact again, ocular communication, it never stops, but this time with the beady eye of a barman aware of my stance, and its sufficient duration, and therefore ready and willing to serve me drink. And then I shouted, assertively, but not too assertively. Yes, I'd done a good clean job. The pints were on their way, so I could relax for a while, my duty done. It felt good to do normal things on a Friday night.

I turned back to view the crowd and something

happened – a sudden movement in the immediate vicinity of sexy Mex, a flurry of limbs, and then a solid slap on the face for Mex's most ardent suitor. I couldn't see properly through the massed bodies but it looked suspiciously like a smack on her arse was repaid in kind, only in the wrong place. Turn the other cheek, sucker, I thought. She continued her conversation unfazed, unruffled, her high spirits unaffected by the tasteless effrontery. He, on the other hand, looked suitably contrite, agitated and thoroughly stupid, gurgling into his pint for cover. Poor penguin. Forced to surrender all romantic aspirations and commence the long lonely shuffle to the deep dark ocean of rejection. I chuckled a bit, happy and amused for the first time in what seemed like ages, and her eyes, good-humoured, registered my response. So I was drawn in again. Christ, was this going to be a process of elimination? If so, I wasn't interested. Or maybe I could speed things up a bit just to see what happened, if the opportunity arose, which seemed likely.

It arose in due course, almost exactly as anticipated.

She was definitely the type to do her duty at the bar, unlike the numerous prehistoric shrinking violets, mocked constantly by the Lads, who had yet to understand modern bar etiquette and its responsibilities, engendered by the new age of equality. Eventually and inevitably, she moved to buy some drinks, all charm and responsibility, slithering through the crowd. The penguin sea parted a little and the allotted path led to within three feet of the Lads and myself, propped innocently at the pumps. Striking distance. If I was going to do something, I had to do it now, so I took a discreet backward step in the required direction. Suddenly and totally unexpectedly, I was out on a limb, exposed. I felt like a teenager, awkward, self-conscious, ambushed by my own nerves. What was wrong with me? I started shaking again. It was a long time since an encounter like this had come my way, and I wasn't up to it. The last few days had obviously rattled me more than I'd realised.

Also, I have to make something clear before we pursue this sorry tale any further. I am not and never was a fully fledged Lad. I tried, and tried hard, for a while. I almost qualified after many years of apprenticeship but something always held me back. I hung in there, nevertheless, as much as I could. Even though I got married at a relatively early age and gladly performed my husbandly duties, I managed to maintain a fairly stable relationship with my vast nebulous group of drinking companions. I was relatively happy with my lot, and went my own relatively unassuming way, straddling both camps relatively successfully. Relatively successfully, that was, until my charming wife banished me from her solid brick-and-mortar camp to the other, more makeshift, encampment on the sea-swept shores. The Lads, of course, by their very nature, hardly registered the readjustment and simply accepted that I was more in attendance than before, and therefore back in line for full membership. Most of them had gone through similar experiences, rarely mentioned, and were always ready to accommodate a distinguished honorary member. It was a lost and bewildered soul indeed who could not reapply after an absence, such were the lax codes of conduct and the powerful flock instinct for keeping the lonely cold at bay. However, regular fishing, chasing women, was expected, even demanded, from full members. This was my dilemma. This was my stumbling block. I never had much need for it until the Wife threw me out. Therefore, at that particular moment in time in Nooks bar I was not only readjusting to extreme circumstances, I was distinctly and patently out of practice when it came to the fishing game.

So, I struck very badly. She bent forward slightly to investigate the possibilities behind the bar, when I slid over beside her and, through a complete lack of anything, not a syllable, in the way of words springing to mind, I slapped her on the butt. It was an awkward, downward glancing blow that immediately brought a flush to my face, in advance of any retaliation. It was an amateurish, feeble, debasing and debased, useless gesture of inept bravado, not even close to the confident, full-handed, cheerful sort of slap that would indicate a similar disposition in its executor. It was, in its pathetic level of gaucheness, like offering a cold, limp and bony-fingered handshake to a hard man of substance and repute from the backstreets of west Belfast. I could feel my mental faculties starting to shut down out of sheer embarrassment, as she turned her head to me in slow motion.

'Do I know you?' she said, matter-of-factly.

A stupid question, I realised, even with my limited grasp on the situation. An RUC man, with a big policeman's nose, once asked me the same question when he stopped to investigate me changing a flat tyre in Queen Street. I asked him how the fuck would I know if he knew me, was I a mind-reader, and I thought he was going to give me a good old-fashioned police battering. Normally, I would have brought this story up by way of reply, but I was under pressure. So I answered the easy way.

'No.'

'Then why did you slap me on the arse?'

She continued, against all the odds, to be plain matter-of-fact. I just shrugged my shoulders and stood there and looked dumb, I suppose, so she answered herself with some more questions.

'Impulse? Couldn't help yourself?'

Corny, but true in a way, and she gave me a little lopsided smile. I smiled back after a fashion. Maybe she just didn't realise the full extent of my bungling failure, or else she was a good actor, in which case she was definitely after something. Or else she was completely pissed but didn't show it, like a true drinker. Or else it was true that arty types have a different way of looking at things. Retrospective analysis, always a minefield. The main thing was she didn't hit me, unlike the other bonzo, and I managed to use my few seconds of silence to regain some mental control.

'Buy me a drink,' she ordered, and then, noticing my blank look, turned all sugar-coated candy. 'Ach, go on,' she said, leaning forward to heighten the drama.

I steadied myself. I tried to calculate the possibilities. I'd just bought an early round. In doing so, I had entered into a contract of sorts, which, to the uninitiated, might have seemed disadvantageous to me but, in reality, was sure to reap eventual and profitable rewards. I didn't need any further complications, and funds were not to be wasted on long shots. I'd suffered too much to get the money I had tucked away safely in the back pocket of my jeans, and there was no way that I was going to spend any more of it in a situation like this. Unless, of course, I had some guarantee of an immediate return, or, at least, better odds that something interesting would develop. I thought for a second. The solution was obvious.

'You're getting a round already. Why don't you buy me a drink, and I'll get the next one?' I said. I tried to make it sound reasonable, but I didn't really expect a reasonable response.

'OK,' she said. No hesitation, no arguments. Very reasonable. Another narrow escape.

She adopted the stance and was served within a few seconds. She ordered a pint for me along with a mishmash of cocktails and trendy beers, and then stood sideways in silence as the drinks arrived, giving the required opportunity to have a good look at her. She could tell that I was suitably impressed, even though I was giving nothing away. Instinct, probably. I could tell that she could tell. Learned behaviour, most definitely. She smiled sweetly at the barman as she paid, and with a little 'Back in a minute', she slipped off with a clink of bottles in the direction of her cronies. A quick return for the rest (no helping hand was forthcoming, I'm afraid to say) and off she went again.

I stood quietly for about five minutes, watching my pint disappearing in rapid gulps far away in the vast mirrored space behind the bar. Suspended in front of the mirrors, rows of spirit bottles and crystal glasses on clear polished shelves caught the light in multiple convex and concave ricochets of colour and counter-colour. The sparkle and glint reminded me of something magical way back in my childhood, something multihued and tinged with brightness. I began to think of downtown lights and big shop windows ablaze with colour, and buses splashing by, crammed with people. Happy days. Christmas in June at Nooks hotel.

I was almost surprised when Mex reappeared beside me, carrying a small leather bag and a bottle of beer. We both looked for a while at my empty glass.

'Want another one?' she said, eventually.

'Of course,' I replied, and that was that. Less than an hour earlier I was dodging punches in a seedy pub. Now I was in the company of a delightful young lady, confident, attractive, and prepared to buy drink. And the night was but a pup.

the wife

My troubles, my little blue period, my travails in the icy ocean, my Stygian crossing, only really started when the Wife threw me out for drinking too much. I know this is a hackneyed, trite and abysmal literary cliché, but, unfortunately, it happens to be true. And, as this is a true story, with names changed, of course, to protect the innocent and foolish, you will have to bear with me for a while as I try to twist my wretched little cliché into something interesting – try to inject some semblance of *jouissance* into the telling, perhaps, or some caustic bite into the narrative, what little there is of it, or a dose of penetrating psychological insight. Believe me, I'll do my best.

I know only too well that the world-weary figure of the typical drunken sod, failed husband, and hardened cynic appears everywhere in literature, movies and common folklore surrounding the base city of Belfast. He is, without doubt, our most popular character in fact and fiction. From a sociological point of view, we could say that this city has produced more of these creatures per any unit of measurement you care to apply than any other city, anywhere. Even the dogs in the street, as the journalists continue to say, know this. Belfast is bingeing and the casualty rate is high.

But us *roués*, emotionally wrecked and ruined but always ready for the next party, represent a strain of culture vital to the lifeblood of this accursed place, and we will not be intimidated by literary snobs, nor held to prescriptive conventions concocted by chalky intellectuals. I am what I am and this is this and I will tell my story as it happened.

From the beginning of our marriage the Wife used to wear a black mask to help her sleep. It was similar to the Lone Ranger's but without the eye holes. It was not a sexual gimmick but was used sometimes as such with me pretending to be Tonto. Its main purpose was to block out the street lamplight that filtered through our cheap bamboo blinds and lined lengthwise our matrimonial bed with a pinstripe pattern of demarcation. It drove her nuts when I tried to count the lines to prove conclusively that she hogged the bed.

The mask, and its similar replacements as it wore out, remained a part of her nocturnal attirement even when, years later, we eventually changed the blinds to something more substantial. She said it eliminated, at least, the horror of my night-time countenance and added that a gas mask would also have been beneficial for the elimination of alcohol fumes. Earmuffs too, maybe pink ones, I suggested, to counter my alleged snoring. A pretty sight indeed for a kind husband about to retire for the night. I bought her a nearly new gas mask from one of those army surplus stores around Smithfield, but she threw it into the corner when I tried to slip it on to her head while she slept. I was gentle enough but I must have disturbed her dreams of the real Tonto in his buckskin drawers. Anyway, around that time I reckoned she was losing her sense of humour completely.

We started off well enough, young lovers matching drink for drink, good-looking and gorgeous, doing the rounds, part of a galaxy of good-time Charlies, always on the go, always finding something to celebrate, ignoring the daily news assault, the guns and bombs, the chilling murders, the dodgy politics. We had to, in those days, or we would have been sucked into the sickness all around us. She was always good with money and always kept a job, always reported for duty, always went to work, no matter how bad the hangovers. We met in a drunken spree and we married in a drunken spree.

I was hijacked on the street while I was in a delicate frame of mind and coaxed inside the local church by the parish priest, a loud and enthusiastic bore, just before the wedding. He lectured me for ages on the responsibilities facing me in the days ahead. Deep and demanding responsibilities they were, not just towards wife, family, Church and country (the country with the big border running through it), but also towards the very fibre of my fibrous soul, in mortal danger from the evils of a reckless and feckless life style. Fornication and drink were the demons he drew upon, knowing nothing about the dope, speed and acid that frequently found their way into my skinny body, and fogged my youthful mind.

I would have fallen asleep if it hadn't been for the good Saint Patrick and the gawping snake under his daintily slippered foot. The painted plaster statue in the corner of the chapel was fading a bit in colour and the crudely modelled robes showed a smattering of flaky white chips at the edges. It stood sidelong to, but well within, my field of vision as the gombeen priest droned on. The snake's head, just about level with mine as I sat stony-faced on the hard holy bench, was a highly imaginative rendering of reptilian agony – bulging eyes, screaming mouth, devil-ishly forked tongue, and flaring nostrils. I didn't know that snakes had nostrils until then. The saintly slipper on the left foot had him pinned down remorselessly at the neck (I didn't know that snakes had necks either) while, four feet above, Paddy's greenish eyes gazed into the far distance, forming a blessed vision of his forsaken Welsh hills and the placid sheep thereupon. My gaze, equally unfocused, formed a hazy mist around the reptile's head, and its deathly scream blurred and distorted itself into a hideous laugh of masochistic glee. I smiled in sympathy and, faith of our fathers, my loud and boring friend relaxed a bit in the monotonous fervour of his speech as he realised his words were bearing fruit in my innermost soul. He winked at me in a conspiratorial sort of way as we later said goodbye, as if, together, we had successfully routed the forces of evil.

Weeks later, in the same building, he winked at me again as he performed the wedding ceremony, during some improvised rant about marriage being nurtured by the grace of the Church, and I winked back knowingly. I looked across at my laughing snake and he winked at me as well, so I winked back at him too. Then I winked at the Wife for good measure and, sacred heart of hearts, she hissed a wicked hiss at me that, in retrospect, said as plain as Paddy's pink plaster skin that the fun was over. Unfortunately, I was too stoned to notice at the time and too happily drunk to care. The scene was set. The script was started. The plot was outlined, and it was soon deemed run-of-the-mill, predictable, boring. But it took a long time, over sixteen years in fact, to work through the inevitable denouement. I was too busy keeping up with my own life style to pay much attention to the details. I just didn't notice the real state of our marriage until it was too late.

When the ultimatum came, it was pretty straightforward – give up the drink or ship out. There were no ifs and buts allowed. I didn't really have any choice. The booze was my best friend, so I was ordered to move out of my own home. I didn't get self-righteous or angry; I didn't put up a fight; I didn't plead or beg for mercy; I didn't resort to recriminations or blackmail; I didn't do anything drastic. I remained philosophical. I applied an old Chinese proverb that I was fond of quoting in bars, especially when my drink was accidently spilt. 'We who are made of the stuff of willows bend with the wind.' So, I just bent a little with the wind and went about my normal business, only not as blatantly as before.

The Wife bent even further, though, and changed the locks. She left a few bags of clothes and other necessary items for me at the back gate, with a formal note attached that told me to please look for somewhere else to live. The marriage was over, it stated blandly. What could I do? The search for an apartment had to begin. And a cheap apartment it had to be, given my meagre resources. I started to ask around the bars for property-type information. The first step was taken on the slippery slope that would lead me inexorably, reluctantly, desperately, more like a goat than a lamb, to the sacrificial office door of the well-known property magnate, the repulsive and slimy Mr Harold 'Biggles' Bigelow.

nooks [2]

Myself and Mex stood at the bar in Nooks and she talked away happily. She seemed to get more bubbly and bouncy as the evening progressed, while I mostly listened and nodded and made amusing comments. I was trying to remain slightly detached, keeping watch on the Lads and the rounds situation and the bar in general. I made sure a number of times, by subtle variations of head and lip movements, that a drink conveniently appeared in front of me just as hers ran low. She noticed the pantomime all right but didn't seem to care.

Nevertheless, I generously explained that the Lads owed me loads of pints but they were a bit tight and I had to continually browbeat them in order to redeem my rightful credit, so to speak. She said she understood, and cheerfully bought herself bottles of beer when necessary.

We continued this ritual for some time without interruption, apart from alternating bathroom visits, hers considerably longer than mine. It appeared that her erstwhile suitors had given up on her, and my flexible drinking companions knew the protocol inside out and would only interrupt in dire emergency. Never interfere when serious fishing was in progress, was one of the unwritten golden rules.

She was the biggest flirt I'd ever come across. Nothing outrageous, mind you, but she was good at the obvious little things – running her fingers suggestively up and down her beer bottle, clinking it against my glass every chance she got and saying 'Bottoms up' with a big cosy smile, pulling out the top rim of her low-cut dress just enough to cool herself down, and leaning forward for regular close-up confidences in both my ears, leaving my eyes free to check out the worn fabric on her bra straps. The bra itself kept peeping in and out from under the dress, which also seemed to possess a life of its own in the way it crept up her bare legs, even though it wasn't tight at all. I could see why some young penguins might feel the urge to slap her backside every now and then.

She chatted enthusiastically about all kinds of crap, and I helped out when I could but I was careful not to give anything away about myself that would lead to complications. I told her my name and occupation and not much else. A man on the run has to be careful. She told me a fair bit about herself. She confirmed that she was indeed an artist, so nothing more needed to be said about my piercing acumen and my razor-sharp analytical abilities. She was an installation artist, who, obviously, installed things in galleries and the like. She talked about some video projection work she'd done, something to do with identity and mirroring. I was curious about that because I had a slight fixation with mirrors at the time and I fancied playing around with some video equipment if I got half a chance. She said something about an exhibition of photographs she was having very soon in town. She also mentioned a few galleries I'd been in once or twice and some artists' groups that I often had occasion to visit when they were throwing parties. It turned out, surprise, surprise, that I knew a bunch of her contemporaries quite well, as sometime drinking companions, but I never concerned myself much about their work, if they ever did any – there was little evidence of energy expended unnecessarily in that direction.

My knowledge of the art world, her profession, as she called it with some irony (I hoped), was all based on gossip and hearsay and resentful bar-room blathering about unfairness and lack of money. My work, only part-time and with very little evidence of energy expended unnecessarily there either, involved writing a column in a local magazine. I had to attend music gigs, sometimes literary readings and festival events, but never art exhibitions. Some other bozo covered that field, not very well, judging by the flimsy copy he handed in. It was even flimsier than mine, but less patronising, and I sometimes had to skim through it in the office as part of my despised editorial-assisting duties.

Needless to say, most of the information she buoyantly imparted to me went in one ear and out the other, but my ears fairly pricked up (and I hope my tongue wasn't hanging out) when she informed me that she lived alone in a large, comfortable, self-contained apartment very close by. I started to order her a drink but she suddenly let out a little yelp.

'What's up?' I asked, confused.

I thought I'd shocked her by my surprise offer, but she didn't answer immediately. Instead, she grabbed at her left shoulder blade, a bit melodramatically, I thought, as though she'd been stabbed or something. But then melodrama was never far away from female inebriation, according to the vast majority of people I would drink with.

'My bra's come loose,' she tittered, reaching round at an awkward angle to correct the fault.

What was a man to do in a situation like this? Nothing much he could do. So I did just that and watched to see how she would cope with the situation herself. She giggled a bit and wriggled about and then, after a cursory explanation, she disappeared into the crowd towards the loo, holding herself front and back.

I used the free time to check with my fellow drinkers, and with some fresh arrivals from other establishments near and far, whether anyone had spotted two big fat men with red faces and ginger hair anywhere. Most of the company were already aware of my predicament and would have normally warned me of any danger but the night was wearing on, and wits and memories were not as sharp as they would have been earlier. It was also in my interest to let as many acquaintances as possible know that I was being violently threatened by lunatics, probably paramilitaries, because of some inoffensive comment in my magazine column. That would serve a much more useful purpose than telling the truth, in terms of eliciting sympathy and possible help. The whole penguin population would have to be told for maximum security. I also used the opportunity of Mex's temporary absence to reposition myself further along the bar, closer to the corner, for more privacy and because the Friday night crowd was packing in tighter and tighter, jostling for space.

Mex reappeared, relaxed and smiling, minus the peeping bra straps.

'I threw it out,' she said, 'it was done.'

I was very impressed. I rewarded her with a beer and we got back to business. I was paying more attention now, keen to hear about the apartment, and I was watching her breasts move in time with her voice and her cute little beer-guzzling noises. The patterned summer dress she was wearing was light enough to allow for the impressions of her nipples to sit prominently on the fabric, and loose enough to emphasise the mild undulations, the quiverings, underneath, as she laughed and ligged about.

I suddenly wanted to touch her or kiss her, but I remained the perfect gentleman. I listened patiently to her as she quickly and enthusiastically jumped tracks in the conversation and started to ramble on about this and that arty stuff, and the peace process, and the political situation, and how artists were busting their asses to help. We were both drinking fast and I realised that the alcohol was taking over, as she was getting more and more animated. So I tried to calm her down by interrupting her and asking about her apartment, over and over again, probably too much, as my own level of mental control began to slip. Who else lived in the building? Where exactly was it? Which floor was she on? What was the rent? Was it very private? Easily accessible? Was there a fire escape? Did she have many friends calling? Did she have a dog? Did it bark at fat men? Everything was starting to telescope in time.

She became quieter and a bit defensive. She must have started to wonder whether I was a closet estate agent or something, and I knew I'd better shut up and let her continue her ramblings. But I was beginning to get bored, especially with the arty business. She wasn't exactly obsessed about her work, but she wasn't far off it either. So I put my pint down and the next time she moved in close to me to make a point I grabbed one of her earrings and held it, freezing her momentarily. Then I kissed her on the lips. Soft. She kissed back without any hesitation, and before I knew it I was groping all over her. It must have been a riveting spectacle, especially for our immediate neighbours, because some of them started cheering and whooping, just like American tourists. I leaned back and glared at them. They did indeed look suspiciously like American tourists and I realised that summer had officially started, rain or no rain. I told them to restrain themselves, to mind their manners, that they were in Ireland now, and that I hoped they liked water because it would probably rain for another two months, just like the last two months. Some of the people behind them started to laugh and took up the taunting where I left off.

I pushed Mex further into the corner. We started again. I hadn't engaged in this kind of behaviour in a public space for years and I was enjoying the novelty. We broke for air, as they say in the bodice rippers, and I slid our drinks over to the end of the bar in case they vanished into someone else's collection. We continued our romances for a while, not too conspicuous. We stopped for refreshments once or twice. At some stage, I tried to say something about getting more drink but Mex gave me a huge grin and then pulled away.

'Back in a minute,' she said, for about the fourth time that evening. I had no reason to doubt her word at this stage, so I settled as far into the corner as possible, pretending deep fatigue and displacing a few grumbling boy teenagers, who probably shouldn't have been in there in the first place, not a whisker between them. I more or less turned my back on the crowd to ensure minimum interference from anyone, friend or foe, and kept a little cuddly space free against the wall for my happy bra-less partner.

Back she came and gave me another big grin. I grinned back and edged her in beside me. We started to kiss and stroke each other, nothing too sentimental. In fact, there was nothing sentimental about it. It was drunken stuff, pretty basic, but not too slobbery or rough and very enjoyable. I slipped my hand down along her back and caressed her smooth, well-slapped backside. I noticed something radically different from my last exploration in this region, just about ten minutes before. There was a natural looseness under the dress. Instead of a pronounced tactile border line between high butt and low butt, there was a smooth borderless transition – one united butt. I almost cheered like a tourist. She had taken her drawers off in the loo, my beautiful little knickerless angel. She laughed at the sudden pause and my sudden realisation.

'They were done as well,' was all she said, between giggles.

We got back to the kissing. I slid my hand over her hip, down a little along the side of the upper thigh, under the dress, round towards the front, and up again. There was barely room to manoeuvre in the crush. No one could possibly see what was happening down there. I was relaxed, free, liberated from my woes, and completely alert as I drew my fingers slowly upwards, and gently, so gently, touched her coarse little hairs. She closed her eyes. I was about to close mine, and kiss her again, when the lights flashed off and on, off and on, off and on, three times, followed shortly by another brutal sequence, and another. Closing time. I couldn't fucking believe it.

bigelow

Harold 'Biggles' Bigelow used to wear sunglasses all the time, or, more correctly, thick heavily tinted glasses that looked like they came from a jumble sale in the poorest part of the grimiest area of east London. They were nothing like goggles, except in the thickness of the glass, but he obviously believed that they provided huge lashings of street cred. They sat at an angle across his pasty face and dug into the flesh above his ears. Maybe, when he was a child, his mother had used some of the money she'd saved by feeding him dog food to buy him the glasses, and he had grown into them. He had a horrible, whining accent and gave the impression of having adopted all the worst mannerisms from the most obvious caricatures in English soap operas. He thought he was a TV character, Flash Harry meets Mr Big, with a nickname to die for.

He seemed interested in one thing only – making money as fast as possible. I didn't know what else he was up too, but he had a vast chain of recently acquired properties in and around Belfast. He went to great lengths to tell me all and nothing about them when I went to visit him at his poky office in the university area, looking for a cheap flat to rent.

The story around town was that, acting on an inspired hunch or possibly some inside information, he bought outright, with cash in some cases, loads of old houses and flats in bad areas close to town, just before the first big IRA ceasefire. He waited until all the property prices eventually shot up, just after that strange twilight time when the other ceasefires were called and real political change seemed possible, and then he moved his whole operation over from England. He resold the smaller, more disposable units for substantial profits, bought some bigger ones, split them up into scrappy flats with the most basic facilities possible, and started renting them out to dupes like me.

He did all his own business, no agents, no middlemen. He worked alone from his office and from his car. He even drove me around himself to look at a few flats he had available. Within one minute in his company I couldn't stand the sight or sound of him. But the Wife had given me absolutely no choice with her lock-changing, bag-packing, note-writing style of negotiation. Nothing suitable had materialised in front of me as I toured the pubs to seek sound advice about the latest property rentals, and I was fed up sleeping on people's floors. I was stuck with him, or else some other creep of an agent, whether I liked it or not.

The first place he showed me was so dark, damp, filthy and expensive that, as soon as we were back in the car, I was working myself up to give him a foul-mouthed lecture on the history of English landlords in Ireland. I got the first two words out when he cut me short with a tirade against the builders responsible for the so-called renovations.

'Sorry, mate, sorry about that. Fucking builders, I asked them to tidy up that mess. Local boys, know what I mean, mate, fucking useless they are. I should get some people over from the mainland to do things properly. Still, do for the students, won't it, they won't notice the difference, will they? Too busy drinking their fucking heads off, aren't they? As long as they pay the rent, eh, know what I mean? You're not a student are you? Oh, that's right, you told me, didn't you, a writer for some local rag? Fucking builders. Probably fucked off to the pub as soon as I turned my back. Useless cunts. No offence mate, but you lot here drink too much. I'll have to get my boys to have a word with them, only way to get things done around here, none of this legal stuff, solicitors and that, too complicated, know what I mean?' And so on, for the time it took to reach the next flat.

I was too busy preparing and improving my lecture to listen to the rest. I was about to make a second attempt to deliver it when the car shuddered to a halt and he jumped out. He strutted, all elbows and shoulders and jerky movements, towards a nearby doorway and pulled some keys out of his pocket. I sat in the car and stared at his ugliness and his awkwardness, his greasy brown jacket and trousers, his pathetic strut and his mouldy hair, and the whole disgusting brown shape of him. I watched as he pushed the key into the front door and then waved impatiently for me to come on, and I made a decision.

I decided there and then to forget about delivering the lecture. I decided to take the flat, if it was even half-decent, and live there as long as I could, or until somewhere else came up, and enjoy it as much as possible and not worry too much about my landlord's appearance or his conversational style, or his politics, or his boys, whoever they were, or his drunken student tenants. I was going to live there without paying any rent and I was going to wreck the place before I left.

The flat wasn't so good – what a surprise. It was dark with a slight feeling of damp, but it was manageable, and it was a bargain compared to the other place. I knew immediately that the stark contrast in value was part of his tactical play for people like me, in the non-student but lower-income bracket, to convince us of our outstanding abilities to spot a good deal, and then jump at it, like Pavlovian dogs at a midnight feast. The psychology of consumer choice. The dialectics of desperation. I was getting back into lecture mode.

I looked around and sniffed the dankish air. I suddenly realised how much I liked my own home, our home, the house myself and the Wife had rented at first and then bought and fixed up – well, the Wife had paid for most of it, decorated most of it, and looked after most of it, but I had helped out when I could and gave lots of useful advice. I would have told Biggles to fuck off back to his mammy and take his tinted glasses with him; I would have bought a big paintbrush and a tin of paint and gone home to tell the Wife that I would fix up our back room, but I knew it was useless. I was trapped and out of luck. So it goes. I was here and I had made a decision. This is this and that was that.

My new home was a self-contained ground-floor affair, with a small living room, and tiny bedroom, kitchen, and bathroom. I made a joke, more out of habit than wanting to engage any further with the ugly brown specimen beside me, about not being able to swing my cat anywhere.

'No pets, mate. They mess the place up, know what I mean?' he said. The terms were settled quickly after that, with no more delays.

In the end I got nine months out of it. I lost my deposit, which grieved me sorely, as they say in the old songs about similar situations, but I used my grief as a source of manic energy to dream up ways and means to confuse Bigelow and to avoid any subsequent payment. I started off by simply not paying the rent for as long as possible. Then, as soon as I heard from him a few times, I postponed the payments further by phoning his office and leaving completely incomprehensible messages. After a few months he started to get impatient. I changed the locks and told him that I'd been burgled and robbed of all my money because the lock on the back door had never been put in properly. I knocked a few little holes around the kitchen and bathroom, loosened a couple of plumbing joints, and complained about the leaks and the cold. When the builders eventually came round to restore order, I set them against him with exaggerated accounts of what he'd said about their work and their drinking habits. I made some more holes and leaks, followed by renewed complaints about the incompetence of the builders. I told Bigelow they were making jokes about his goggles, knowing that would guarantee long-term trouble. I refused to pay anything until proper repairs were done, and made sure not to be there when the new builders arrived for their numerous visits, at my arrangement, of course. I complained by mail and phone about my deteriorating health. I ignored his angry letters of protest. I implicated the post office in the non-delivery of notices to quit. I kept him busy with bogus phone calls about emergencies and bad repairs in other buildings. I wrote more letters complaining about the conditions and informing him of my solicitor's views on the matter. I only let up when the threats started, warnings about his boys and nasty visits in the dead of night, and possible damage to my balls, and so on.

As far as I was concerned, it was all bluff. He probably didn't have any boys. He was too tight to pay anybody to do the real thing when threats would usually be enough. But it was a good time to leave anyway. By increasing my output in the magazine slightly but noticeably, and by adapting my drinking routines to a more covert operation, accompanied by regular concili-atory phone calls, I'd managed gradually to curry some favour with the Wife. She was beginning to thaw, to become the sensitive, caring, lovely human being who would welcome me back into our nice familiar, warm and tastefully furnished home. She needed only a little more persuasion.

I asked for some respite, for a temporary, yes, definitely, only temporary, sojourn back in the old homestead, in order to repair my ravaged health and to recover from my exploitation at the hands of that unscrupulous English landlord. I knew the last bit would touch her heart strings more than the first bit, so I never shut up about it when I called to see her. I frequently delivered the lecture originally meant for Bigelow to the Wife, to her armchair-republican friends and to her family, with a major shift of emphasis from the perpetrator to the victim. It worked, as I knew it would. Eventually, they hated the word Biggles more than I did.

She gave in.

I made the necessary arrangements to move back home. I phoned Bigelow's office for the last time and left a long message on his answering machine. I told him I'd had enough of his damp, ruinous apartment and his incompetent builders, and was moving to a better flat in another part of town. I said that I'd never do business with him again because his attitude was a disgrace and his properties should be condemned. I told him to keep the deposit, but given the terrible and deeply unjust circumstances under which I'd lived, I could not possibly be held liable for any other payments. I also told him that I was a fair and law-abiding citizen and would naturally return the apartment keys to his office, by registered post, no less, just to make sure he received them in the quickest possible time.

When everything belonging to me was safely removed to my rightful abode, I paid one final visit to the flat where I had endured my lonely but interesting matrimonial break. I loosened the joint on the mains water pipe behind the bath until there was a small but steady leak. I did the same behind the boiler, and then knocked a few more little holes at strategic points to encourage the seepage in places where builders would be likely to cover up faults. I closed the main door quietly as I left, threw the keys neatly into a nearby litter bin, and walked off into the rain to join the Lads for a few celebratory pints in McLaverty's. I was in most excellent shape for a fistful of drink.

I might not have been in such great form had I suspected that Bigelow's boys did actually exist and were soon to be recruited on to my case. Little did I realise in my uncommonly blissful state that, one quiet afternoon in the Star bar about four days later, I would have the surprise pleasure of making their acquaintance, and not only that, but I would have the opportunity to tell them one of my all-time favourite jokes.

nooks [3]

Mex started to laugh, but I shushed her, and told her off. In this particular establishment flashing lights were not amusing, they were an inconvenience, an annoyance, and a trespass on our freedom to enjoy the basic legal rights granted to us from on high. In most other bars on the planet a single flashed light at this particular time simply meant that no more beverages could be purchased, thank you, dear clients and customers, so please make your way to the exits at your earliest convenience . . . but bear in mind that you can stay for a good half-hour or so, by lawful decree, to finish your drinks and any other business you may consider important before we finally and reluctantly have to encourage you to leave so that we can lock up . . . please have a safe journey home and thank you again, and do call back.

The staff in Nooks, however, were either ordered or encouraged by their bosses to rid the bar of stale feng shui as soon as possible. They employed a variation on the Central Belfast Method of removing customers. This was originally developed by the thugee bouncers in McLaverty's and subsequently taken up by rival premises, on the grounds, presumably, that McLaverty's was a very popular bar and therefore it must be good for business to terrorise your customers at the end of the night. The Nooks version of the Method was relatively simple.

They always flashed the lights early, continuously and vigorously, in counts of three, for about two minutes, thus blinding the customers. The staff closed the tills immediately, and then retreated for a while to a small back room behind the bar to allow the fury and wrath to die down a bit. They would then run around and scoop any drinks that weren't gripped tightly and shout at the punters to get out. This was followed by frantic brushing and sweeping around the remaining feet, while the famous blue-blazered doorman deserted his post to help in the onslaught. Transformed by hours of boredom and faked deference from a catatonic lackey into a ferociously nasty fiend, he would snarl and yap at the final few huddled victims. He would roll his eyes and pace about and growl at individuals, or bark at defensive groups, to finish up and leave the premises, or else. He had been known, on some occasions, to resort to the last-person-out-is-barred tactic, the unkindest cut of all.

As far as the current situation with my newfound friend stood, I knew what was coming but I was determined to exploit my novel situation to its fullest extent and to bring it to its natural and fruitful conclusion. At the final flash of lights the bar was completely packed with gulping and swallowing people, most of them dreadfully aware of the imminent débâcle. They were trying to co-operate, being generally good-natured souls, but were naturally unwilling to give up or waste their last precious drinks. Myself and my practically naked companion were concealed in the far corner, away from the exit, by the struggling drinkers. We could count on at least ten minutes, until the crowd started to thin. Even after that, there would be reasonable cover from stubborn desperadoes retreating away from the doors in our direction. I reckoned a good twenty minutes in all of guaranteed privacy.

So Myles and Mex got busy. Away we went again on our private little sexual jamboree, making jam while Nooks gargled.

bill and ben

'Listen. Listen. Have you heard this one? Bill's sitting on the edge of the bed. "Glee, glug-a-lug, glee-glop-a-lug, glug-a-lug, bee-bop-a-Weed," he says. "If you love me, you'll swallow that," says Ben.'

The two fat lumps, who had just recently sat down opposite me, looked into my face with pity and disgust. There were tiny specks of rain on their bedraggled ginger hair and larger droplets heading south on their black bomber jackets, but the fat boys were otherwise concerned. They were annoyed, I could tell. They obviously didn't get the joke. I didn't expect them to like it very much, but I thought, at least, they might understand it. I couldn't help it if certain obvious correspondences popped into my head and I had to articulate them. I couldn't help it if the one on the left had a squeaky voice and the one on the right had a deep voice. I couldn't help it if their almost identical comical appearance – huge black jackets and boots, black baggy trousers, ginger hair and big red faces – made them automatic figures of fun. I didn't care if they got annoyed. I just wanted to let them know, without actually saying so because that would have been too simple, that they were not welcome at my table. There were plenty of empty tables to sit at, and I was having a good laugh with my drinking buddy, telling him about how the Wife had welcomed me back into the fold. But they sat on.

They had appeared out of nowhere, total strangers, in the middle of a quiet Tuesday afternoon in the Star bar, one of my favourite daytime haunts. They said something to the barman, who seemed to nod at me. I had never seen them before, so I was surprised when they came over and planted themselves down in front of myself and the mate. They leaned forward like bad men in a bad movie and told my sidekick to take a long piss. I told him to stay put but he said politely that he needed a piss anyway.

They introduced themselves, kind of informally, as friends of Mr Harold Bigelow, my ex-landlord of some days' duration. More accurately, they said, they had been dispatched by Mr Bigelow, and designated the unpleasant task of locating me and informing me of my position vis-à-vis their honourable employer, or words to that effect, delivered in their own inimitable manner. They had spoken in turn, squeaky voice first and deep voice second, and then the same again, and had seemed set to continue in this vein when I so rudely interrupted them with my apposite little joke.

'You listen, dickhead,' said Bill, 'this isn't fucking funny.'

'You're in deep fucking shit,' said Ben, eyeballing me severely, like he was practising for an audition.

'We're going to keep tabs on you for a while, until you start paying Bigelow the money you owe for the rent and damages,' said Bill.

'A lot of fucking money,' said Ben.

They went on a bit more about knowing all about me and where I hung out, and then about the Wife and what I was up to and how they were going to make sure I did what I had to do, and then all about the terrible fucking things that would happen to me or the Wife or some of my mates if I tried to fuck off or anything stupid like that. They took turns without looking at each other, as if they had been doing this all their lives. I wasn't really listening to them. I was fascinated by how they managed to share out the idle threats more or less equally without any cues. I reckoned they must have been twins, not quite identical, born into a long line of mountain dwellers, trained like monkeys and imported to the city for jobs like this. But I didn't get a chance to quiz them about their background, or to tell them any of my twin jokes.

I was just about to tell them to relax, that it was all right, that I would contact Bigelow and sort it out within the next week or so, when Bill must have noticed my lips parting a fraction, hesitating, just about to speak, maybe to tell another joke. He stamped his big black boot on top of my more flimsy model, right at the front of my foot, hard heel on soft toe. Then Ben slapped me, not too hard, but immediately, quickly, on the side of the mouth to stop me howling.

'You better sort this out, fuckhead,' said Bill. 'Or we're going to have to hurt you. You know where to get Bigelow.'

'You've got a fucking week, that's all, before we come looking for you,' said Ben, taking his turn.

They both stared hard at me. My head suddenly cleared for the first time all day. This wasn't funny. This was fucking serious. I'd managed to get myself mixed up with a pair of violent, mind-reading, wind-swept flowerpot men from the mountains, who didn't like my jokes, or who didn't understand them, what difference did it make now? A splendid choice of joke too, well done Myles, your sense of diplomacy was outstanding. I felt stupid. My pride was hurt even more than my toes. I became acutely aware of eyes everywhere locked on to our table. I felt even stupider.

I made a frantic grab for my pint to steady my nerves, and my fingers had just made contact with the cool glass when Bill slapped it across the table and onto the floor. I think that's what scared me most – the way they read the moves so quickly, so easily.

The buddy had just appeared back from his nicely timed piss, when the twin mountain men, without further comment, rose up simultaneously in front of him. Bill gave him a little shove back out of the way as he approached the table like a sheepdog sneaking up on some troublesome sheep. Ben marched to the door and held it open like a true gentleman, and the flowerpot men both disappeared in a puff of smoke – one of the more unflappable punters at the end of the bar had given the proceedings a fitting finale by blowing a lungful of cigarette smoke in their direction as they left. I could tell by his scowl and his near-empty glass that he was expressing his disapproval of Bill wasting good drink.

I was going to give off to him for trying to make matters worse but decided, instead, to shout at the barman for touting on me. I hollered at him. My behaviour was so threatening that he just shook his head, called me a fucking eejit, and asked me did I want a pint on the house, or what? Of course I did. Dead right. I slumped back into my seat.

As the other punters mumbled and grunted among themselves and nodded in my direction, the barman whistled to himself as he brushed up the mess.

The mate sat down and bombarded me with forty questions. I ignored him. I waited for the free pint and brooded. When it came I gulped at it nervously, shakily. Then I brooded some more. I needed to work this out.

Things had suddenly taken a turn for the worse just when I was getting on top of them. I remembered that the Wife had mentioned two large men calling at the house the day before, looking for me, but she said that they were very friendly – polite, she probably meant. I thought they must have been promoters trying to use the personal touch to get me to write something nice in my column about a new venue or something, so I didn't worry about it. It had happened before. I hadn't written anything that could be called nice for a long time, and my grumpy editor was complaining that I should be more positive, what with all the peace talks and everything happening. He had also told me about a phone call, a male caller who wouldn't give a name, asking for my current address, but I'd forgotten all about it within ten minutes.

This was not good. The Wife was my first concern. She might have to be informed, partly informed, that was. Basic information only. I was only supposed to be staying with her temporarily, but the thought had set in my mind that, as time rolled on, she would almost certainly relax a bit and allow a gradual and romantic progression from the guest bed to the more comfortable main bedroom. And then, happy days, Myles would be reinstalled, king of the castle once again, a reformed and dedicated husband and living companion. I didn't want to fuck that up. What could I tell her? Anything but the truth, so help me God. But would she find out what had really gone on with Bigelow, I wondered, if I didn't tell her anything?

The mountain men would probably visit her again, and again, and sooner or later, yes, she would find out. And she would see it in simple, practical terms – that I spent all the rent money on drink. I would be unceremoniously thrown out, never to return, with no comeback, no comeback at all, not a leg to stand on. None of my fairy stories could cover this situation. Unless I got it covered now, right away.

The Lads would have to be told to divulge nothing, to look out for two crazy fat bastards with ginger hair and red faces asking stupid questions, and to keep me informed of their movements and possible whereabouts. Barmen would have to be coaxed or, heaven forbid, bribed into silence. Ignorance of anyone of my description would have to be the order of the day. Christ, I might have to avoid my usual habitats for a while or change my appearance, or both. Paying the money to Bigelow was out of the question. There had to be other alternatives.

The buddy blabbered on about getting some of the Lads to fix the flowerpot men, but I knew he was raving and sent him to the bar to get more drink, another free one for me, if possible, and one for himself. The Lads, to a man, would run a mile rather than get physical with the likes of my persecutors – unlimited cheek, certainly, and verbal run-around, but no fisticuffs, thank you very much.

I needed somewhere to hide that very few people knew about, to lie low for a while until this thing blew over, as these things always do. Unfortunately, I would probably have to be out and about. My miserable part-time job demanded that I attend various gigs and events, and I couldn't risk losing the work, boring as it was. But I would be careful, vigilant, move stealthily, prove that I couldn't be intimidated. I could handle it. I was a man, not a mouse. I was trying to convince myself, but it wasn't working. I was fucked, and I knew it. Then McNabb came to mind.

The buddy set down two pints.

'Free? No. I knew that miserable bollox wouldn't give me another one.'

I swallowed my drink back in a few quick gulps and arrived at the only possible solution. I would go to McNabb's and hide out. I would tell the Wife nothing until

I talked to him. I made up my mind to collect some of my things, only the really necessary bits and pieces, as soon as I could. Sometime when the Wife wasn't at home. Then I was going to pay my old friend McNabb a visit. I hadn't seen him for ages. The flowerpot men couldn't possibly know about him. He was the main man. He would help me out for sure. That was it. I calmed down a bit.

'Fuck them,' I said. 'I'm going to get another pint.'

'Cheers,' said the buddy, settling into his seat, thinking everything was back to normal.

nooks [4]

I stepped in closer to where Mex was standing. I pushed her slightly backwards, tighter against the wall. I slid my right hand slowly down over her breasts, lingering a while on the nipple imprints, then on down over her belly and hip, then underneath the dress. I slipped my middle finger into the wet centre and slowly back out again to lubricate her. Jam-making was indeed an art and she was proving to be a great little artist. She installed her long slim tongue against the roof of my mouth, encouraging me to suck at it. She moved in time with my slippery finger as it built up its momentum, as it rotated and circled and grazed and smoothed to the peculiar rhythm of genital pleasure. Her hips hardly moved backwards and forwards at all, in terms of distance, and her belly hardly moved up and down, but they moved, they moved enough, and they did so with instinctive purpose, alive, receptive, inviting.

I opened my eyes less and less frequently, and turned my head less and less often to monitor movement in the bar, as we smooched our way into an alcoholic, animal smoulder. I lost track of time and became only semi-conscious of the noise and commotion around us. Everything was warm and wet and moving in one slow steady oscillation. My head was spinning slowly, with a hazy glow playing on the inside of my eyelids. My finger was gliding in rhythm with the glow and with the swaying softness pressed against me. My cock must have been hard, or hardening, but I was just vaguely conscious of it. The awareness was all in the finger and brain, and, in the background, the hot, generalised, sensate motion of rocking to and fro.

My little artist, my little Leonarda of jam production, started to gasp and grunt and heave against me, and her hands tightened on the back of my neck. She groaned a long low groan, not loud but from deep within, and I opened my eyes to look at her. Her mouth was wide open and her eyelids half-closed. Her hair had been pushed backwards and it looked like it was standing up on end, as if she had been electrified. She reminded me of my mother, when I was a child, coming out of the bedroom one morning after making some strange weeping noises, all flushed and flustered, pushing her hair back and shouting at me about what was I looking at, stupid wee nosy parker, go and play somewhere. I knew at that moment in Nooks, as the image faded, that I was either in love or in deep trouble.

Mex collapsed against me, away from the wall, and started to laugh. We slid sideways along the bar a few feet as I tried to keep steady and hold her up, and I noticed an acute lack of resistance from other bodies or stools or anything else. I froze for a second. Then I swung round and there we were, in a small open space, surrounded by a tight semi-circle of grinning onlookers. Right at the front, dead centre, and the only one not grinning, was the Wife.

She hit me an almighty smack on the mouth, which, at least, prevented me from saying anything stupid. She stormed off through the gathered assembly of punters and penguins, who were all certainly having a great night of free entertainment. The grins disappeared and the assembly dispersed rapidly as the blue-blazered wonder arrived on the scene, screaming that time was up. He took one look at us and he stopped hollering. I was slouched against the bar like a bad Shakespearean actor hamming it up, holding my mouth, which must have been bleeding slightly, as something tasted salty. And Mex was slouched behind me, equally Shakespearean, I imagined, with her dress twisted around her, her face and hair scorched and electrified, her bare butt probably half-showing.

'You're barred,' he hissed through clenched teeth.

'Fuck off . . . sir,' I retorted, more from the shock of being caught red-handed than anything else.

He made a grab for me and I punched him right on the chin. It was a straight, instinctive jab with very little force, but he jumped onto it and then fell to the floor without a sound.

There were cheers and clapping and laughter and general penguin noises as I grabbed my coat from a stool, then grabbed Mex by the wrist, and she grabbed at her bag, which had been lying on the floor, and we pushed and bumped and bobbed our way out through the bar and into the foyer. I could hear a familiar female voice shouting 'Bastard, bastard' in the background somewhere as we swept out through the main door. The Wife was still there. Even more reason to move quickly.

One of the Chinese owners, obviously assuming that we were rushing to catch friends who had just boarded a taxi in the street directly opposite, was holding the door open in lieu of blue-blazer. He smiled and said, 'They're waiting for you. Good luck.'

mcnabb

The fuss over the mountain men and the spilt drink soon died down, and the Star returned to its usual humdrum business of gossip and smoke, bets and booze. My buddy settled himself down for a bit of a session. I pretended that everything was all right. Some of the Lads drifted in and were told various versions of what had happened, depending on who they listened to. The buddy maintained that he had been keeping a keen eye on the proceedings from the toilet entrance, just in case he was needed. The barman claimed I was insulting two innocent big fellows from the sticks, by the look of them, with my fucking awful jokes. I told them very little. I just asked them to be on the look out for Bill and Ben, described in similar terms by every witness, even the barman, as two big fat pigs with red faces and ginger hair, and to warn me of any sightings.

Before I got too drunk I went to the public phone just outside the pub where it was quiet. I phoned McNabb at home to make an appointment to see him. That was the way he worked. He was surprised to hear from me after such a long time but he agreed to see me the next evening, because I told him it was important. His place at seven o'clock.

I spent the night at the buddy's smelly kip of a house, just to be on the safe side, and because I couldn't face sneaking into my own home as a guest at two o'clock in the morning, only to be dragged out of my visitor's bed early the next day to be quizzed relentlessly about my recent nocturnal activities. I was sure to look guilty and the Wife was sure to notice, as she always did. She was sure to badger me around the kitchen and living room, not allowing me to settle anywhere for more than five seconds, and I was sure to break down and tell her the whole story just to get a drink of water and an aspirin for my hangover. She wouldn't care about my fat tormentors and why they were pursuing me. She would blame everything on me. And she was sure to kick me out, there and then, because of my pathetically stupid and selfish ways, and so on. And I wouldn't have time to collect my necessary bits and pieces, and I would end up at McNabb's all bedraggled and confused at seven, and he would be totally unsympathetic. And then I would be completely buggered, up shit creek without a paddle, as I used to say in my younger days before I discovered more subtle clichés. So the buddy's it was.

I fell asleep eventually on the bumpy sofa. I woke up in the middle of the night to have a piss and, as I staggered blindly along an unfamiliar, cluttered corridor towards the bathroom something leapt, screaming, out of a doorway behind me. The light flashed on. My heart jumped against my ribs and I crashed over sideways with the shock. As I fell I banged my forehead loudly on a shelf, positioned perfectly to obstruct any downward movement in the narrow hallway. The buddy, bare and skinny with baggy pink Y-fronts clinging to his hips (just wait until his mates heard about this), kept screaming at me – something repetitive about Jesus, Mary, and holy Saint fucking Joseph. I knew this was only a preamble to something even less meaningful, so I screamed back at him to shut up and help me back to my feet. Other screams started to emanate from his bedroom, and it took a while to sort things out.

He must have been even more worried about the fat men than I was. He said that he'd hardly slept all night and that his girlfriend kept kicking him for waking her up with his tossing and turning. His nerves must have been well and truly frayed by the time he heard strange bangs and gasping noises in the corridor. He imagined, some-how, that we had been followed home and that I was being strangled. I told him I always made loud expectant noises on my way to the loo and that he should tidy up his corridor a bit if he wanted some peace and quiet. He went back, grumbling and scratching, to his insomniac torture. I slept well after that, knowing that he was so vigilant.

He threw me out without any breakfast. I told him I would be back with all my stuff to stay for a few days, but he didn't respond, not even a smile. He just closed the door quickly behind me. I could hear his girlfriend shouting at him about something as I walked away.

After a quick breakfast at my favourite diner, where I met a few mates who'd been partying all night and had the cheek to insult me about my appearance, I called into the office of our esteemed publication to catch up on things. Decent of me to weigh in was the general response. I managed to type up some riveting rubbish to keep things ticking over for a while and then disappeared before any complications arose. I spent the rest of the day at home alone, my lonely halfway home, my ex-home, with the Wife safely and resolutely at her place of work. It was raining too hard to go anywhere except into a nice cosy pub, but I had to stay reasonably sensible. I lay in the bath for hours and pondered. I rehearsed my story for McNabb over and over, adding little details as I went, just to make sure I would get his full and complete attention. He was a busy man, after all, with those government schemes and intricate plans he was involved with.

I didn't actually know what he was up to most of the time but it must have been important. I knew from various snatches of conversation over the years that he had become some kind of troubleshooter within the civil service. He didn't talk much about his current position. He was some kind of behind-the-scenes mistake-spotter and supervisor for senior civil servants employed to facilitate high level political discussions. He never engaged directly with anyone in particular, as far as I could figure out. He scoured documents and proposals and pointed out contradictions and incorrect assertions, and the like, through discreet memos and notes. It was all cloak-and-dagger stuff but he always made light of it and never mentioned specifics. This arrangement was fine by me because it meant that, on the rare occasions we met up, we hardly ever had a serious conversation. I could tell my latest jokes and stories of low-life scandal, and he seemed to enjoy them as a kind of healthy antidote to the pale limbo of exactitude he had found himself in.

I was confident he would help me; that is, let me stay in his house for a while. He would help me because he had always helped me before when I needed something – a guarantor, a small loan, some mortgage advice, occasional feedback on my column. And because we had history. I had saved his life about fifteen years before. It was no big deal on my part (and I modestly never mentioned it again until now) and he knew it, but it had created something between us – a bond of opposites rather than a debt – that was long lasting and not subject to the usual conditions of demand and response.

I had literally bumped into him for the first time in the Lock bar on a busy night. I had never come across him before. He was completely drunk and kind of aggressive-looking, staring at people nearby and then trying to focus his eyes on the clock high up on the wall, then back to the staring again. People were shuffling nervously around him, trying to avoid his gaze. I didn't like the cut of him. He looked like a deranged cop. I was trying to sidestep past him to get to the bar when he turned suddenly and we knocked against each other.

'I'm going to kill myself,' he mumbled into my face. 'At midnight. I'm going to drive into the river at twelve o'clock. Through the railings out there, into the river. I'm going to drown myself. I'm going to get in the car and drive into the river and drown myself. Or maybe I'll walk. Too dangerous to drive in my condition, eh? Ha, ha.' A drunken cackle, forced, derisive. 'What do you reckon, eh? Eh?'

I didn't reckon anything. I'd heard all this kind of drunken crap before, so I told him a joke.

'Two fleas are going out for a drink and one says to the other, should we walk or take the dog?'

'What?' he said, obviously dumbfounded, appalled by my lack of sympathy. Tough shit. He should have picked on someone else. He gawked at me with his mouth open, his eyes blinking in slow motion.

'What?' he said again.

I told him the joke again, even though that's not my policy. Once is enough, I always say. If they don't get it first time round, too bad. Just like life. But I felt sorry for him.

He stared at the clock for a while, as I chuckled at my own joke and tried to catch the barman's attention. Then he absentmindedly set down his drink, a double or treble whiskey, and weaved slowly and carefully out of the bar.

I lifted the whiskey, and followed him to the door. I watched through the partially etched glass as he crossed the dark, half-empty carpark. He made his way eventually to a big black-looking car parked under a round yellow lamp. The car was positioned at an odd angle, facing directly on to the flimsy, rusted metal railings that separated the carpark from the steep bank of the Lagan. If he goes in there, I thought, he won't need to drown, he'll die of some unknown disease.

He managed to get the door open and hauled himself into the driver's seat. I sipped the whiskey. Black Bush. Very nice. Long time since I'd had one of those. Every cloud has a silver lining. I drank the rest of it in little steady backward sips as I watched him rock his head backwards and forwards, his face catching the light on the forward movement and then disappearing momentarily into shadow before reappearing again and again, yellow against black, yellow against black. The car didn't start. It wasn't midnight yet.

I left him to his manic head bobbing and went to the bar. I told the flea joke to a few faces close by as I waited for my pint. They laughed and grinned and raised their glasses and everything was grand. There was nothing wrong with my jokes. I went over to the door again and looked at the black car. The deranged occupant was throwing up through the open window, spewing a thin stream of gunge down the side of the car door, yellow against black. I soon lost interest. Yellow and black always reminded me of my old school tie and there I was trying to have a good time. I went back to swap some jokes with my new friends at the bar.

I got a nasty jolt about an hour later, just before closing time, when an upright, sober replica of the midnight dipper tapped me on the shoulder and asked me politely if I wanted a drink.

'Of course.' My stock reply. He got me a pint and a coke for himself.

He thanked me for what I'd done. He told me that he'd gone off and had something to eat and that he felt much better. He then presumed unfairly upon my precious time and upon my agreement to have a drink with him. He spent about twenty long minutes telling me about his job grinding him down and taking him nowhere, and his wife and family leaving him, and the usual stuff about nothing working out the way you plan it, and so on. Then he kept repeating that he was now going to take control of himself, or something like that. He couldn't have realised that by this stage of the evening and partly thanks to his earlier contribution of one very large whiskey I was completely smashed. He might as well have been talking to the cold, black river that he was so desperate to join in final embrace not so long ago.

I spent years trying to piece together the odd remembered fragments and key points of information imparted in those twenty minutes, but even with some background details gleaned from members of his family during infrequent conversations and chance encounters, I'd never been able to fully comprehend the reasons for his completely untypical suicide urge. Neither had I been able to work out exactly the role of the flea joke in his miraculous recovery. I could only speculate that the McNabb flea had a sudden revelation, an instant satori, that he could, in fact, somehow walk the dog of his unfortunate circumstances.

When I arrived at his house promptly at seven o'clock on the evening after my brief sojourn in the buddy's house, I didn't know how he would react to my predicament. I was clean and sober, hopeful and optimistic, but also prepared for the worst. What I didn't expect was that, after listening to my miserable story, he would tell me more about himself in one hour than I'd managed to find out in fifteen years. Neither did I expect his invitation to stay as long as I needed, in the comfort and safety of his stylish home, under certain conditions, of course, nor to be taken to task about my spiritual condition and to be advised so dramatically on the only way forward. A complete spiritual renewal, it seemed, was the only solution to my problems.

mex's place

'Where are we going?' shouted Mex, as we skidded down the steps in front of Nooks, kicking up water as we went.

'Your place,' I answered, 'where else?'

'OK,' she said quietly.

'Well, which way then?' I had to ask.

'Round the corner, there, to your right.'

We trotted at a quick pace until we were out of sight of Nooks, around the corner, and then we slowed down, gradually coming to a halt beneath a low, arched streetlight. I looked around. Nothing much going on except the usual drizzle. I let go of her wrist to rub the knuckles on my right hand, painful from the punch on blue-blazer's chin. Mex slumped back against a nearby hedge and spread herself against it. For some reason she started to rock sideways, to and fro, laughing, soaking herself in leafwater and splashing it all around the wet pavement. I felt something stir inside me that hadn't stirred for a long time. She came to a halt and I looked at her, propped against the hedge, grinning. The warm rain sparkled and fell around her, catching streaks of pale orange light from the streetlamp overhead. Her dress clung to her, and the light accentuated and exaggerated the curves and crevices. Her hair, now flattened and shiny, glistened and her earrings bounced silver against her skin. Her eyes were little dark slits of amusement, shadows of delight.

She was sort of half-panting, and she curled out her tongue to catch the fiery raindrops. What a flirt, what a ham, what a completely enchanting little performer. It was too much, too much for anybody, certainly too much for me. My shiny little jam-maker, near naked and dripping with light, I had to have her, there and then. I moved in close to her and she grinned right at me. I lodged myself tight against her and we kissed hard. I forced my hand between her legs and she caressed my suddenly bulging cock, cramped and corralled and pushing uncomfortably against the inside of my jeans. She started to tug at the zip.

A bunch of drunken rowdies came carousing around the corner, singing and chanting and swigging from beer cans,

and momentarily distracted us with their leering comments and unsightly gestures. How dare they, the uncouth
hounds, the scurrilous dogs? I recognised some of their
faces and made a mental note to seek retribution at a more
appropriate time. Mex responded more pragmatically and
pulled me roughly into a pathway and then behind the
hedge she had been leaning against. We were now hidden
from the street in a little light-speckled shadowy space,
tightly bounded by the dark side of the hedge, backed
against an unlit curtained window.

We kissed and grabbed at each other. I unzipped my
jeans and her hand immediately reached in and levered
out my dick, hot and hard and aching for release into the
wet air. She squeezed and stroked it, not with force but
just firmly enough to encourage the slow ache to quicken
into something more imperative, like a tight spring that
had to be released. Before I knew what was happening,
she had swivelled around and bent over, and was steering
my cock into her from behind. Expertly, with both hands,
one in front beneath her, the other looped round over her
backside, she guided me in. I flipped her dress up out of
the way and it swung lightly from around her waist. I was
in a shadowy heaven, wet and wonderful. I could feel the
pressure in my cock building up as I pushed and pushed
into her.

There was a sudden flash of movement and a rush of
shadows. A metallic growling noise pulled up on the street
beside us and we both froze. For a few terrible, gasping
moments I felt the pressure drop, the spring loosen a little.
The car, with headlights beaming, had swung onto the
kerb at the other side of the hedge. It sat with the engine

running quietly, lights now switched off. I knew that no one could see into the dark space, but it broke the spell, the magic rhythm. I could feel the slackening in my groin and I imagined the dreaded brewer's droop invading my system right at the moment of imminent release. I cursed inwardly and squinted at the little leafy shadow-faces closing in all around, ready, it seemed, to taunt me.

But my handy artist was indeed a talented little rearranger, a sensitive and skilled little fixer, an installation artist of the utmost expertise. She performed a simple twist and pull as she backed against me and, Bob's your uncle and Lily's your aunt, we were once again locked together in deep and secure communion, moving into full locomotion.

We rocked away in the dark drizzle and the leafy half-light for a few ecstatic moments, and then I paused for the second time as a sudden wave of sober concern washed over me. Again, my shiny-wet, bare-arsed companion noticed the slight hesitation, the faint aberration of rhythm, and read my mind.

'I'm on the pill . . . it's all right, it's all right,' she gasped quietly, between low breathy groans. 'Go on, go on . . .'

Such glorious talent. She leaned forward a bit and arched her back some more, taking the weight on to her hands, which I noticed were now spread evenly on a stack of bricks located conveniently beneath the window. I wrapped my hands around her hips and moved her forcefully backwards and forwards as I regained the steady rhythm. On and on I went. Her feet shifted sideways, outwards, creating the splendid, illusionistic, compliant impression of allowing more depth for my penetrations.

I caught sight of myself momentarily in the dark space of the window as my head rolled sideways, twisting with the irresistible mixture of delight, aggression and freedom of this unexpected, delicious, drunken fuck. I briefly acknowledged the concentrated, translucent Myles who glanced back at me. I closed my eyes for one long, last lunge before the climax arrived.

Everything went white in my head as the rush exploded silently, and the breath was forced out of me from below. The only thing I could feel for a while was my own soft, self-conscious bite into my lower lip to help stifle the involuntary noises – the deep, rolling groans that gradually subsided and transformed themselves into throaty gasps and nasal hums.

The car on the other side of the hedge suddenly clunked into gear and took off as noisily as it had arrived.

Mex and I remained in our coupled, panting, breathless position for a few minutes and listened to the traffic and the voices and the howls and raucous laughter of the streets around us, ebbing and flowing in random patterns. We silently watched the shadows of passers-by crisscross the patterns of our dank little haven. I felt transformed.

Mex straightened up, her dress slipping down immediately to its rightful position, and I clumsily, and slightly painfully, started to put away my diminished and sticky little member. I almost pretended to ceremoniously wipe it clean on her dress before tucking it in – a faked, comic gesture, based on a bad joke about what Irishmen do after sex, that I once developed with the Wife into a little act that was guaranteed to elicit playful screams of horror and slaps across the shoulders – but a second thought caught me on.

'Who was that woman?' said Mex, slowly smoothing herself down and looking at the ground.

Uh-oh. Here we go. She didn't waste much time. I could have said anything, but I didn't. I told the truth.

'My wife. We're separated.'

'Why did she hit you, then?'

'I don't know. I don't even know why she was there. Maybe it was the shock of seeing me perform such an altruistic act.'

'Is that what it was?'

'No. For fuck's sake, I was only joking.' I told myself to be careful with the jokes.

'I'm dripping,' she said.

'Yeah, so am I.'

She laughed, and I felt great again.

'No you're not. I mean, I'm *dripping*.' And she stood up on the sides of her feet briefly, and then lifted them one after the other, looking at the ground.

I laughed a little nervous, embarrassed laugh, though I was absolutely sure there was nothing to be embarrassed about. Gravity is gravity.

'It's good for the weeds,' I said suavely. 'Let's go.'

She smiled and lifted up her bag. She stepped out into the light, moved away from our shady sanctuary past a low adjacent wall, and turned into the short pathway next door. She took out a key and opened the door.

'Come in,' she said, and disappeared inside.

I followed along, dumbly. What could I say? At least we didn't have to walk in the rain, which was becoming heavier now in the still-warm night.

I followed her up the stairs, dripping water everywhere, through a lighted doorway into a hall. This led into a large, well-lit, spacious room with an open kitchen on one side, situated behind a wide work surface. There were no pictures on the walls, which surprised me, apart from a group of small photographs bunched together in one corner around a designer-type lamp on a thin stand. The varnished wooden floor, and the low, sparse furnishings, along with the carefully spaced lighting, gave the impression of considered choice, order, and even a hint of money. A long table at the far wall was covered with papers, letters, books and notebooks, piled around a phone, and a narrow recess close by was filled with colourful books and magazines.

Mex pulled the heavy, floor-length curtains across the bay window, turned towards me, and mimed a little here-we-are gesture with her hands. She went to the kitchen, got me a bottle of beer from the fridge, as I stood and absorbed the cosy atmosphere, and then she vanished into the hallway. I noticed a hi-fi system on a shelf in front of a long plain mirror near the kitchen area, but I was too lazy to search for appropriate music. I just threw my wet coat over a chair and slouched into the low settee and sipped my beer. It occurred to me to look around for possible signs of a regular male presence, or at least a frequent visitor. And for some reason I half-expected a dog to leap out at me, but I was too tired to care and too happy with myself to worry about such trivial matters. All I had to do now was be nice, listen a bit, not tell any jokes and not fart too much, and everything would be all right. My luck had to change sooner or later and maybe this was the big break I'd been waiting for. If Mex concentrated on the sex and didn't talk too much, we would get along fine, and maybe I could stay for a while, but I didn't want to make too many plans all at once.

I contented myself with lying back and being conscious of not having to go to McNabb's place, of not having to slip in quietly and tiptoe around and be soberly careful. I kicked my boots off, and I felt like taking off all my clothes and lying naked on the settee with my sticky dick glued to my pubes as a kind of memento mori for the old days. But I didn't do anything except drink my beer and stare happily at the ceiling, and feel pleased with myself. Some pup, our Myles, some pup indeed.

When I woke up the beer bottle was no longer in my hand, there was a small blanket half-draped over my legs, and my neck was sore. The lights were still on, but no sign of Mex. I checked my watch. I'd been asleep for about two hours. I staggered to my feet and into the hallway. The bathroom door was wedged open and the light left on – very thoughtful, no unnecessary staggering about in dark corridors here. I felt tired and still a bit drunk, but I was very happy to find myself in this situation, being looked after as a welcome guest, with no conditions, for a change. As I relieved myself, a bit too noisily, stallion's stream and all that, I noticed the shower was still wet, and her dress was hanging from a hook above a damp towel on the floor.

I washed my hands and face at the sink. I noticed three toothbrushes in a glass, but that didn't necessarily mean anything. I looked at myself in the mirror. Strangely enough, I didn't look too bad, apart from the red eyes, the little purplish mark still lingering on the forehead, and a slightly swollen lip. I smoothed back my hair with some water and looked along the shelves level with my face. A man's razor, but that didn't necessarily mean anything either, sat neatly among the usual stack of strange skin lotions and potions and jars of white stuff. Not much evidence of anything, really, except that she was very careful about her skin, which, of course, should always be encouraged.

Two more doors led off the hallway, one closed, the other half-open. I pushed gently at the obvious one and it swung fully open, revealing, in the light from the hall, a small study with a desk and bookshelves crammed in tightly against one wall. All the other available wall space was covered almost entirely with Polaroid photographs and scribbled notes. In the other room my cute little artist was undoubtedly sleeping soundly in a big double bed with a generous space left available for the handsome visitor, who only happened to fall asleep through having too many sleepless nights, and not through lack of interest or too much booze. Before I joined her, I decided to have a quick nosy around in the study. No harm in that. The door was open, after all. I reached in and switched on the overhead light.

Mex must have been a busy woman with all this paperwork everywhere, but there seemed to be a fair degree of efficient organisation. The desk was covered with neat piles of letters and notes, and a small computer, sprouting a sheath of yellow Post-its, was wedged into the corner. I thought artists never bothered with this kind of boring bureaucratic rigmarole. I was under the impression that they unceremoniously dispatched all paperwork to the bin. In fact, the poor artistic creatures I was familiar with gave the impression that they couldn't even spell paperwork, or work for that matter, and couldn't afford a stamp. Maybe she could give me lessons in desk management sometime. We could even go shopping together to help me pick a nice desk lamp, like her elegant little chrome model.

I turned towards the Polaroids on the nearest wall. These things were expensive. Yet there must have been hundreds here, mostly simple photographs of faces or couples posing for the camera, distributed more or less evenly across the surface of the wall with a few gaps here and there. It looked like Mex wasn't short of a few bob. I moved round them slowly, scanning the faces. I didn't know what I was looking for or why, maybe to catch her posing with some handsome git, or in case I knew some of her buddies. I was just curious. I heard a distant, muffled groan, followed by a faint snoring sound. She was fast asleep in her bedroom, bless her little cotton socks.

I continued to scan the photos, absentmindedly, half-heartedly – they were boring, full of people afraid to smile, arty types being cool. I stopped and yawned, and was thinking about having a shower before slipping in quietly to join my conscientious and talented friend next door when I noticed, among all the generalised organisation, an even more carefully positioned group of images on the other wall.

I stepped towards them. Their arrangement suggested a dominant, special role among the general plethora of images. As I moved closer, I could see that they were full-length portraits of pairs of people, some male, some female, and some mixed, but all pairs. I stooped even closer and I could see that each pair looked like twins, mostly identical, staring blankly at the camera.

Something sparked my attention, a subliminal flash of recognition, and before I even realised what it was, my heart thumped. My eyes raced across the ordered rows and columns to one central point.

Fuck, fuck, fuck . . . fuck.

Near the middle of the group there was a sunny portrait of two fat, red-haired, red-faced bastards standing in front of a redbrick terraced house somewhere. I pulled it from the wall and some pins bounced across the floor. I held it up to the light. There was no mistaking their ugly mugs. Jesus, Mary and Joe, what were they doing here?

I leaned backwards and dragged the only seat available, a solid wooden chair, across the polished floorboards towards me, and sat down underneath the light. I stared at the photograph for a long time and swore under my breath. It was them all right. The fat fucks. I heard a noise behind me and looked round. It was Mex, in a big white T-shirt with a double Elvis image printed on it, squinting her eyes against the light.

'Matt?' she said.

'What?' Did I hear right? I turned round a bit more. 'Who?'

'Oh, it's you, Myles. Sorry.'

mcnabb's place

I arrived at McNabb's at seven, as arranged, soaked from the heavy rain. He welcomed me with a warm hand-shake and a distasteful look at the torrent of water I was introducing on to his perfectly maintained hallway floor. How was it possible, I thought, for him to make me feel genuinely welcome and immediately uncomfortable at the same time? No one else could do it. Behavioural dialectics, maybe that's what we had in common. Then again, maybe not. Unlike myself, he managed to walk the middle line. He was always diplomatic, even when he was being brutally direct. He glanced at my forehead.

'Nice bruise you have there, Myles,' he said, sympathetically. 'Pissed last night, were you? Must have banged your head on a shelf or something sharp, by the look of it.'

A bad start. I intended to use the dark reddish mark as evidence of the seriousness of my plight. I was going to flaunt it as an example of the sort of punishment meted out, merely as a preliminary warning, by the vicious brutes on my trail, even before I'd had a chance to pay back any of the tiny amount of money I owed. I could feel my carefully fabricated and well-rehearsed version of events, designed to gain maximum sympathy, slipping from my memory already.

Feeling a bit ill at ease in one of his luxurious armchairs – the type you sink into and can't get out of – I more or less told him the truth about my unfortunate circumstances. I decided, after the first sip from the whiskey he handed me, without bothering to ask what I'd wanted, that it was counterproductive to lie to him. If he agreed to let me stay for a short while and then found out that I had been spinning him yarns, he would almost certainly bounce me out.

Myles the Rubber Man, that's what things had come to, trapped in someone else's armchair, afraid of being bounced, and feeling so sorry for himself that he had to tell the truth. That's the way it goes. This is this and that was that. So the truth came out, in most of its pathetic detail, and I must admit I didn't feel any better afterwards for my painful efforts, just a bit more exhausted from the telling. I started near the beginning, about nine months before.

He had only met the Wife a couple of times in all the years we'd known each other and he seemed to like her, at least he got on very well with her. So he frowned a bit when I described how the marriage had been terminated by her official decree and how I had been ousted from my castle with no legal rights. He had, after all, helped us with the mortgage arrangements when we decided to buy the house, in the Wife's name only, unfortunately, because she had a full-time job. He had also strongly advised us at the time to draw up proper documents in case some such problems arose. Which we neglected to do, of course, despite the Wife nagging me for years to do something about it for my own benefit. He frowned even more as I described Bigelow and the flat, but then, surprisingly, he burst out laughing when I told him about the damage I did. He smiled and nodded knowingly throughout the builders and the repairs and the final non-payment of rent episodes, which I embellished just a little because of the favourable response.

After the embarrassing bit about Bill and Ben in the Star bar, he rose and poured some more whiskey into my glass. Then he sat back and listened intently as I ran quickly over the rest and summarised by telling him that I needed somewhere to hide out, just for a while, and that I had nowhere else to go.

He asked me about my job and how much extra money I could earn. I told him it was a crap job, part-time, and didn't pay very well, as he knew already, but that it suited me fine. I said that I wanted to keep it more or less as it was. I pre-empted his next question by stating bluntly that I had no intention of paying any money to Bigelow, under any circumstances. He laughed again, and took a big slurp of his whiskey, which he'd been sipping at pretty steadily. Then he spoke to me in a subdued, level voice, the way he might speak to some young inexperienced civil servant who was about to enter the lion's den with a ruthless twister of a politician intent on making trouble.

'All right, Myles, you can stay here as long as you need to, at least until you get some sort of resolution to the situation as it stands. I'll pick you up in the car tomorrow at your place during the day and you can bring whatever you need back here. You can have the spare room upstairs and I'll give you a key to the front door. There are some conditions. Don't tell anyone, not even your wife, that you're staying here. Lie to her, if you must, but if anyone calls here or phones here looking for you, you're out for good. She is the only one who knows me and might guess where you are, so be careful. You can come and go as you please but not too late at night or if you're totally pissed. Set the house alarm any time you go out and don't write down the number, it's easy to remember. Don't go into my study upstairs or into my bedroom and don't mess around with any papers or documents that might be sitting around. Don't answer the phone or the door; in fact, don't use the phone at all, and if I ask you to disappear for a while when my family or anyone else visits, I'm sure you'll understand. The front door is hidden from the road, and the side gate is almost invisible from anywhere, so it should be easy for you to slip in and out unnoticed. The neighbours know the score with me, so they won't bother with you, even if they do see you around.'

I liked the part about lying to the Wife, if I must, and not bothering with the neighbours, but not much else about the conditions. But I said nothing and he continued with the same broad, steady voice.

'You'll need to be careful at work as well. Don't accept any registered mail in your name, and tell the people in your office to do the same. Bigelow will probably have a solicitor trying to trace you, as well as the heavies. How you deal with those two Bill and Ben characters is up to you, but violence won't work and they'll keep coming after you as long as he pays them to, or until someone discourages them. That's where I might come in. I'll do my best to help you out but I'm busy all the time now, and I may not know the right people for this job. But we'll see what can be done.'

I really didn't know what angle he was taking here. He was assuming that I knew a lot more about his work than I actually did. I knew practically nothing about him, when I thought about it. I started to regret not listening properly to him all those years ago, and he must have noticed some slight change in my demeanour, or a subtle shift in my body language. He paused for a few seconds. I tried to fake some positive signals and smiled weakly.

'You know it's time you started thinking a bit about your life style, Myles, and I don't mean just the drinking. What age are you now? Thirty-nine, isn't it?'

I was taken aback. How the fuck did he know that? I reckoned I was in for the whole heap now, the full harangue about my all too obvious failings and nothing about my obvious qualities. I didn't think my main man would stoop to the same level as the Wife, not to mention her mother and her nosy sister and her nerdy brothers. I didn't answer. I was suddenly disappointed with McNabb, but he confounded my paranoid expectations and immediately changed tack.

'I'm ten years older. You know what happened to me? You know why I'm still here, doing what I do? That first time we met in the Lock I was in a really bad way. You know most of the details. I was drinking heavily for the first time in my life. My wife had gone off with someone else, someone less demanding, she said, and taken my three kids with her. We'd just moved in here and I had to cope with fixing up this place by myself and paying off the mortgage. My job was killing me with boredom and frustration. I was drawing maps in the Ordnance Survey branch of the civil service for years and they were holding me back, obviously because of my background. They had all the details on file. I was brought up in a republican family in west Belfast. I had a degree in History and English, one of the few Catholics to even get to university in those days, but I couldn't get a job anywhere after I left college, so I ended up training as an ordnance surveyor with a bunch of eighteen- and nineteen-year-olds. They were mostly really stupid but well-turned-out kids from middle-class Protestant homes, the sort of homes where bigotry was disguised by a polite veneer of respectability – you know, the sort of people you used to ridicule in your column.'

Me, ridicule the Protestant middle classes? Of course I did. And why wouldn't I? I used to ridicule everybody, every chance I got, until my spoilsport editor decided to butt in and ruin everything. The cutting edge of ridicule, that's what my column was, and that's what the readers liked. Then I was put under pressure to change it because of the so-called peace process. Hardly fair, now, was it? McNabb looked at me hard. My concentration was beginning to drift already, but I managed an amused nod and he continued.

'I got so fed up with the map-drawing that I started to put in little details that weren't supposed to be there. No one noticed the deliberate mistakes, even though there was supposed to be a double-check system. I suppose they prided themselves so much on their stringent training methods that they never reckoned on something as mundane as an error of draughtsmanship. It was innocent at first, the odd tree or house or church symbol thrown in here and there just for idle amusement. But as the years went on and everyone else was promoted to better work in the department or out in the field, it became my only way of hitting back. I started to get compulsive, neurotic, about it, screwing up the maps deliberately. It was a very petty and degrading way to get revenge. I became more and more edgy and bitter, and afraid of getting caught. My marriage started to fall apart, mostly because I was so bloody fussy about trying to get everything else right. Then I hit the drink.'

I deliberately winced here, right on cue, and he smiled a little ironic smile. I swallowed the last of my whiskey, and he good-naturedly poured me some more, but noticeably less than the last helping. He gave himself another large shot, just to be sociable. He was more focused on himself now, and I tried to relax and enjoy the privilege of catching up on what I was supposed to have known already.

'And when I met you in the pub that night, I really was going to finish it all. I knew that if I went into the Lagan in a locked car, I'd never survive. But what you said about people being fleas feeding off the system, riding the dog, whatever it was, must have struck a chord. I snapped out of the fog and I started to think that I could use what little I had to feed off the system a lot better. I was just a small inconsequential part of a corrupt and ugly institutional setup, but I could still exploit its weaknesses.'

So much for my jokes, I thought, but at least he remembered part of it. And this was getting interesting at last.

'I took some time off and got myself straightened out. I thought a lot about the whole business and gradually realised that it was all a game, a game of interdependency, that we were all parasites feeding off something bigger, and that it was possible to influence things right at the highest levels by a gradual and constant irritation of the system at the bottom . . .'

He was talking my kind of talk now. I wanted to cheer him on or something, but I knew what kind of reaction I'd get.

'. . . So I started back on the deliberate mistakes, but this time systematically and with a view to the bigger picture. I used every opportunity and every excuse – bad timing, sick days, rushed jobs, faked ineptitude – to transfer my distorted maps over to my fellow draughtsmen to finish so that they would sign their names to the completed work. They didn't like it at first, and it wasn't officially supposed to happen, but we had all done it from time to time to help each other out. Eventually they got so used to my incompetence and my stupid pope-head ways that they started to patronise me and bale me out of my predicament, just so they could boast about it among themselves. The smart-arse fenian with the degree knew his place, and kept his mouth shut for a long time.'

He paused. There had been a slight trace of bitterness in his voice, not much, but some. He must have realised that I'd noticed. He took a second or two to regain his composure, and then resumed the steady delivery.

'Then, inexplicably, I suddenly appeared to become the most assiduous and efficient mapsman in the department. I started to spot mistakes everywhere. I constantly reported, to my immediate superiors, minute discrepancies in plans I had come across in the files. The reports increased quickly and the more mistakes I found the more nervous people got. The result was gradual promotion, and, within a short while, I was delegated the responsibility of searching through everything produced in the department for possible errors, or even sabotage. I was soon given a team to work with and then, eventually, I was made responsible for restructuring the entire training procedure. The funny thing was that, over a period of time, I actually produced a much more efficient and effective system. You know what the secret was?'

I was tempted to say an injection of humour, or longer holidays, or an influx of loose women into the office, but I could tell that McNabb was getting into his stride and that he should not be interrupted with stupid and frivolous remarks. Normal penguin patterns of social interaction did not apply here. I obliged him and shook my head dumbly.

'Everything was duplicated at source. Everything was done twice by two different people, or, later on, by two different methods. Costly but effective. And you know what I discovered?'

Another dumb shake of the head. I really hoped this wasn't going to turn into a session of twenty questions, like I used to get from the Wife. Rhetorical questions were her speciality. And my neck was always sore from the incessant nodding and shaking that was necessary to convince her of my earnest attention.

'No two plans, or documents, or maps, or anything else, drawn up by two different parties were exactly the same. So I changed the agenda. Instead of pretending to aim for perfection, I looked for errors through duplication. In a nutshell, instead of trying to prove the maps right, we tried to prove them wrong. And what did we get?'

Christ, only seventeen to go, or was it sixteen? There was no telling how long this could go on. My neck would be fucked. I came to a quick decision. I made no attempt to move or make a sound. I just listened.

'A more fluid and more accurate map-making system than ever before. And it was in place long before we got computers and location satellites and the rest. It's still in operation now, to a large degree.'

A thin, tight-lipped flicker of a smile was all he got in recognition for his outstanding achievements. He took a quick sip from his whiskey and continued, undaunted.

'The more I thought about the duplication thing, and the inbuilt discrepancies, the more it made perfect sense, and it applied to everything, not just work. I realised the obvious – that the investigation of reality through any system automatically involved both the distortion of that reality and the compromising of the system. Every fabrication, every duplication, is naturally a deception. The understanding of any so-called reality must therefore entail a pattern of deception, and so reality, as we know it, is a deception. So, no two people are going to see things exactly the same way. It seems trite in retrospect but, at the time, it was a major personal and professional break-through for me. It freed me to a large degree from trying so hard to get people to see things my way. I became detached.'

I was listening very carefully to all of this, but my head was getting sore, not my neck. Maybe I was the one who was trying too hard to see things his way. Perhaps, after all, I was right not to listen the first time round. I was getting confused – not by what he was saying, which was pretty straightforward gibberish compared to some of the drunken nonsense I was used to listening to, but why he was telling me this stuff, at this particular time. My enduring image of McNabb the Modest was beginning to wobble and distort. I thought he was finished when he stopped here to take a long gulp, but no such luck.

'Ironic, isn't it? By messing up the system I worked within, I was able to turn it around, change it. As a result, I was eventually encouraged to search for flaws in other departments. And, hey presto, a load of promotions followed. In the work I'm involved with now, the methods we've developed to crosscheck information, compile documents, and even estimate the prevalence of certain opinions, are more reliable than ever. Our negotiators are briefed more efficiently and the way we assess their results leaves little room for distortion. It's top level stuff. There are a lot of important changes happening at the moment. I'm involved with the new security arrangements, some tricky work, could be a bit dangerous. I can't really talk about the ins and outs of it, but the beauty of the operation for me is that I can do most of my work from here, from my study, if necessary.'

Jesus, what had I stumbled into? Top secret security activities, peace process negotiations and Assembly talks and Christ knows what else, and here's the man in the middle, who likes an audience to talk about himself and his work when he's had a few drinks? I was getting ready to say thank you very much, Mr McNabb, sir, but I think I'll be on my way, if you don't mind, when he laughed at something. I must have screwed up my face slightly.

'Don't worry, Myles, everything's duplicated at my office. I prefer to work there most of the time, so you can still come and go without any bother. But you can see why I have to emphasise the conditions imposed on you. Don't touch any of my bits and pieces, especially upstairs. It's very important for me that everything stays in order.'

'Of course,' I said. The whiskey was kept downstairs in the kitchen, so I wondered how stringent the conditions might be in that regard. I made a mental note to enquire later, at a more opportune moment, about the house etiquette in terms of guests helping themselves to drink, and maybe even some food.

McNabb gradually slowed down a bit with the patter. But he continued to talk about his work in a more general way for quite a while, and then about his busy life style and so on. I was feeling kind of stunned but settled, when he suddenly leaned forward, frowned significantly, and changed the subject completely. He delivered his *coup de grâce*.

'You know, I think you should cut down on the booze and look for some extra work to get the money to pay off Bigelow. That's my honest opinion. But it's really none of my business. I could give you the money, but I don't think that's a good option for you. I have to be blunt. You need a change, Myles, some sort of new model for your life, a complete spiritual renewal of some sort, and I don't mean that in a strictly religious sense. I think that it's your own responsibility to find a solution for yourself. I mean that if someone gave you the money to sort out this problem, you would have nothing to fight against, nothing to keep you going. It would be like spiritual suicide. What do you reckon?'

What could I say? I held out my glass and tilted it towards him at an angle.

'Can I have some more spirits to help me on my path? Or, as the Buddhist said when he went into the pizza joint, make me one with everything.'

He laughed and laughed, and I ended up laughing too, despite myself, for the first time all day.

'Can I stay the night?' I asked, while he was still chuckling.

'Of course,' he said.

mex's place [2]

I sat under the light and stared at the Polaroid photograph of the mountain men, and wondered who Matt
might be. I was suddenly tired. Very tired. As tired as I'd
ever been. Too many questions were buzzing around in
my brain and I didn't want to deal with them. I needed
to sleep.

'Got any whiskey?' I asked Mex. She was still standing
in the doorway, squinting her eyes and rubbing at them.

'Listen, Myles . . .' She started to explain something, but
I didn't want to know. I threw the photograph of the fat

red fucks onto the floor in front of me, and asked her again, politely.

'Have you got any whiskey?'

'No. Just beer and vodka.' I could tell by her voice that she was still drunk.

'Get me a glass of vodka, will you? Straight with no ice.'

She disappeared into the main room. I rose from the chair and walked slowly into the hall. I had a passing look into her bedroom, but couldn't see much in the narrow light from the hallway – just a duvet thrown back across a low bed, some clothes lying around a chair and the dark shape of a wardrobe in the background gloom. No more surprises in there, at least. I could hear the sounds of clinking and pouring and quiet cursing going on in the kitchen area as I passed into the living room.

Mex handed me a glass as I sank into the settee. She stood and watched as I swallowed the vodka in three or four quick gulps. I was going to down it in one, just for effect, but I was feeling delicate and there was too much of it. I shuddered a bit. I hate vodka, but I wanted to knock myself out quickly.

'Matt, whoever he is, won't appear tonight, will he, unexpectedly, like?'

I looked up at her as I asked the question, and she looked right back at me with no trace of anything, just dark, tired, empty eyes squinting at mine.

'No. But he'll probably be here tomorrow. I'd like you to . . .' She hesitated.

I thought for a second that she was going to ask me to leave, and I turned my head away sharply and let out a little melodramatic sigh of vodka fumes. She had obviously witnessed some similar performances before, for she quickly said, 'No, I mean . . .' and hesitated again. I turned the glass around in my hands and examined the speckled pattern on the base. Not very stylish at all, really. A bit kitsch, in fact.

'I mean, I want you to meet him . . . Tomorrow, maybe. I'll tell you about it in the morning. You can stay the night, if you want, no problem . . . Do you want to come to bed? I'm knackered.'

How very fucking decent of her to ask, I thought, but not much point if she was knackered.

'No, I'll sleep here,' I said gruffly. 'Near the fridge.' The questions were starting to come back, with a full battalion of reinforcements. I wanted more vodka.

She laughed a bit and, again, surprisingly this time, it made me feel better. I decided to forget about the vodka, and I lay back slowly on the settee. I was too tired to go anywhere or do anything. I pulled the blanket lazily from the floor and wrapped it around me. Yellow and black, the colours of depression. Yellow and black tartan, with little red lines to liven it up. Fuck it.

'Good night,' I said. I forced a half-smile at the ceiling. She switched off a light somewhere.

'Good night. See you in the morning.' I thought the tone of her voice suggested some degree of disappointment, but I told myself not to get so full of it. The door closed. I was relieved to be left on my own and I squirmed around until I found the most comfortable position under the tartan.

I lay for a while and nothing happened. No sleep, anyway. Nothing but questions and more questions. The Matt mystery was starting to bother me, but it was nothing compared to the Twin mystery. The Wife mystery was hovering between the two. What was she doing in Nooks, anyway? The Flatfield mystery lurked in the background somewhere, as if the strange events there had happened weeks ago instead of hours ago. The possible repercussions of the Nooks débâcle weaved their way into the fabric. I couldn't care less about being barred, but the lanky bouncer knew who I was, and he might talk to the cops.

On top of everything else, the Mex mystery circled and twisted in my head. Who was she? What did she want? Did she feel the way I felt? Why should I meet this Matt wanker? An image started to form in my mind and wouldn't go away – a tall handsome bastard, young and stylish, probably with loads of money, trendy as hell and full of arty shit. Sensible and sober too, no doubt, the miserable bollox. I liked Mex, and I wanted to be with her, for a while anyway. Matt would have to fuck off out of our lives and stay fucked off. I would have to meet him tomorrow and mangle his young, trendy ego with my ferocious wit, superior knowledge and hardwon experience. If that didn't work, I would persuade him to go for a drink and threaten the crap out of him as soon as Mex was out of sight. Unless he was a really big fucker, of course, in which case I would have to drink him under the table and make an eejit out of him. It was me or Matt. Do or die. This is this and that was that.

I could feel my brain bubbling with all this volcanic stew, and my head was starting to spin. The questions were rolling round faster and faster, and images of the Wife ranting at me to wise up and catch myself on flashed into the jumbled mess. I could hear her taunting and teasing me. Grow up. Act your age, you irresponsible, juvenile asshole. Middle-aged delinquent. Useless, drunken shite. Failure. Loser. Matt will be here tomorrow. You'll be humiliated. Dumped. Chucked out. Loser, loser, drunken shite. Loser, loser, drunken shite . . .

I began to wriggle and writhe and kick with anger and frustration, and pull at the blanket this way and that. I was going to kill the bastard when I saw him, the skinny, interfering arty fuckpig.

There was still a lamp left on somewhere in the far corner of the room, and every time I closed my eyes, the light stayed on in my head, and fizzed and crackled and heated up the stew even more. I struggled to bring my racing, tumbling thoughts under some kind of control but I knew it was too late. I threw off the blanket and stumbled towards the lamp to switch it off. I stopped. I turned and staggered back towards the kitchen area. The vodka bottle was sitting on the work surface, where Mex had left it. It was about three-quarters full. I twisted off the red cap, and gulped at the narrow mouth. I shuddered and coughed and spat and gulped back some more. I leaned against the nearby column of wall that helped separate the kitchen from the main living area, and steadied myself. I put the bottle to my head a few more times and drank and spluttered. I turned, just about to set it down again to regain my breath and pull up a seat, when I caught sight of myself in the mirror above the hi-fi.

Jesus, talk about handsome? I was baggy-eyed, ruffled, blotchy-nosed, pale, pinched, and agitated. I leaned towards the mirror to have a closer look, and I stopped dead. The deep shadows from the lamp across the room made my eyes disappear completely and a sixty-year-old stranger stared at me. He was stooped awkwardly in a baggy black T-shirt and crumpled jeans, and he gripped a half-empty bottle of booze. His features were lined and drawn, and distorted into a kind of rippled mask, stark and austere. He coughed at me a couple of times and the open, shadowy mouth in brief spasm reminded me of something – something like a choked reptilian gasp.

I stepped away in horror and saw myself transformed back to myself, ruffled still, but twenty years younger. I stepped forward and there he was. Back again and there I was. I started to laugh at the magic mirror.

I forced a few more gulps from the bottle, and leaned back against the wall. Everything in the room was twisted and exaggerated by the punctuated contrasts of light and dark, the shadows too deep and the brights too bright. I was starring in my own film noir. The third man would soon appear. The bumps on the walls were swelling out and the furniture was getting bigger.

'Go to bed, Myles, go to bed. You're fucking cracking up.' I was talking to myself as well now, another bad sign.

I had to kill that light, that tall, thin, designer lamp in the corner. I swayed over to it, pulling my T-shirt loose from my skin, soaked with sweat. I was holding on to the bottle with a desperate, slippery grip. I felt myself lurching and belching as I leaned over to switch off the light. I groped around the top of the lamp and scorched my fingers on the hot bulb. Fucking designers, fuck the lot of them. Where did they hide the fucking switch? I banged the bottle down on a small table, and fumbled and stumbled and cursed, and followed the electric cord to a socket and jerked the plug out.

Darkness. A deep, soothing darkness, cancelling out the shapes around me. I stood for a few minutes and breathed it in, quiet, cool, inert, anonymous. I swayed gently to and fro, and then even more gently as I regained my equilibrium. My head was spinning slightly, but it was all right. Suddenly, no more questions. I wanted to stand there all night and sway and spin in the dark, but I knew I had to move.

As soon as I did, the spell was broken. I staggered and banged into something and fell over and crawled until I found the settee. I slid onto the soft, giving fabric and groped for my blanket on the floor. I pulled it over me and curled up. Somewhere far away outside, in the real world, a dog barked faintly, plaintively, a few times and then fell silent.

'Don't worry, Fido,' I whispered to him, 'every dog has his day.'

home

McNabb roused me in the early morning at his place, his home, his headquarters, with a cheerful, but polite, knock on my bedroom door. I was awake already. I was watching the faint, spiky leaf shadows from outside the window move to and fro on the curtains, attacking the floral patterns. I'd hardly slept all night, even though everything was extremely comfortable – the big double bed, the spacious room, the temperature, the level of darkness, even the north–south alignment of the furniture, if I wasn't mistaken.

I'd been thinking about the Wife, mostly, my brain laboriously turning over and over again the same bumpy ground with nothing to show for it in the morning light. I had to tell her something, sometime soon, and certainly not the whole truth, if I hoped to salvage my improved position in her ordered universe. She would have to know that I was staying somewhere else for a while, and that it was useless to ask questions about it. I had to meet up with her. This meant I had to get her on neutral territory, when she was in a reasonably good mood, and without me being drunk, or even close to it. At her house, our house, our home, without any bystanders or witnesses to mutely enforce some kind of social protocol, I would be mauled mercilessly until I gave in and confessed everything. Home was where lies and excuses were relentlessly unpicked and dissected, until the deceitful victim longed for the comforts of the womb. I once left a recruitment form for the cops, with her name on it, sitting conspicuously on the kitchen table. But it disappeared, without comment, never to be seen again. The criminal fraternity never knew how lucky it was.

Neutral territory, somewhere free of acquaintances, drink, or other potential distractions, was hard for me to imagine, but it was certainly possible. The other two requirements were more difficult – her in a good mood and me sober. So it was a tricky situation. When in doubt, postpone, that was my usual rule. But I had to do something. She would be upset about my latest disappearance, especially after the brief spell of civilised companionship and all the promises of permanent change. She would be more than upset, she would be furious. But what could I say, anyway, that would make her less furious? Not much. To hell with it. I decided to postpone.

The flowerpot men had really screwed things up for me, just at the wrong time. Fat fuckers, no point thinking about them, but they slushed around in my consciousness like two tons of festering shit that rose again to the surface every time it was buried. There was another little stagnant pool called work, but I knew I could cover that for a while.

As I came down the stairs McNabb greeted me cordially over the top of his coffee cup. He asked me if I'd slept all right and I nodded. I didn't want to spoil our first morning together. He arranged a suitable time in the afternoon to collect me and my necessary gear from the Wife's place, and then he rushed off to work, reminding me about the conditions, especially the alarm code rule, as he left.

I had some light breakfast and a little think. Then I broke my first condition by phoning the magazine office. No one was there. I left a message on the answerphone, explaining that I was sick but that I would keep tabs on things and that I would post them enough copy to keep my column going. I had a few roughly finished articles set aside, mostly waffle about some obscure jazz figures, that nobody would ever read properly but would still lend the column a gratifying veneer of hipness amongst the other dross. I had kept them in reserve especially for emergencies like this. Clever boy, Myles. Foresight, my mother used to say to me, is what distinguishes humans from animals. When I asked her once about squirrels and nuts, she said sadly that maybe I wasn't so stupid after all. I could feel myself smiling a bit.

Then I phoned the Wife's work. No one was there either,

as I had correctly guessed, at this early hour of the morning. Lazy dogs. They had a rickety old answering machine, which I'd had occasion to use before, and I left an elaborate message for her. I didn't mention my name, in case other ears were first to the phone. I said that something had come up and that I'd found somewhere to stay, that I was picking up some of my things when I could arrange transport and I would sort out the other stuff later on. I told her that I was doing fine, that I was getting on with things, and that I would be in contact soon, and so on. The machine cut me off after about thirty seconds, as anticipated, while I was still talking – thus giving the desired impression of a thwarted urgency on my part to alleviate any worry on her part. A surfeit of information and not enough time, that's the modern way.

I didn't like leaving the Wife in limbo and I didn't like breaking the conditions on my first day at McNabb's place, but it had to be done to save further inconvenience and misery. And what possible harm could come from using the phone once or twice? Anyway, McNabb would never know. Another faint smile.

Then I remembered the number recall facility, frequently used by suspicious characters to access the number of the last person to phone them, and I started to panic. Could it be used to check a call to an answering machine, with only a recorded message to go by? I wasn't sure. It was possible, but only if it was the last message on the machine. I could phone again from somewhere outside, but the nearest public phone around here was probably miles away, and the Wife would be at work very soon. They won't check, they won't check the number, there was no reason to, I repeated to myself.

'Shit. Someone might. Some fucking nosy bastard,' I shouted aloud.

Myles the Moron. Stupid asshole. I cursed myself, the Wife, McNabb, the phone company, every nosy fucker on the planet. I got in such a mental bind that I nearly phoned British Telecom to see how much they really knew about their own sneaky phone services. The sudden realisation that it was too late was a familiar one. My whole day from then on, and it's a long day when you get up so early, was a constant barrage of self-abuse, self-recriminations, pointless regrets, and repetitively mindless questioning of my repetitively mindless behaviour.

I left McNabb's to walk about for a while and try to clear my head. I came across a phone box about a mile from his house and it sent me into a complete dither. It was too late. She would have been at work by that stage, checked her messages and started answering new calls with a cheery good morning and how-are-you-today? I walked past the booth a few times and kicked at stones and twigs and dead bees on the ground. Then I wandered about aimlessly for a long time in a grey drizzle that came and went every five minutes. When would it stop? No wonder the bees were dying. I thought about emigrating, but who would have me? Eventually I started to make my way home, to the Wife's home, I reminded myself. I wanted to have plenty of time to pack everything I needed, so that I wouldn't have to sneak back for any missing articles at a later date. This was the final break. I couldn't see any way around it.

I veered towards McLaverty's at the last minute. The best laid plans were something I knew all about. A few midday pints, I decided in a flash, were the only ready solution to my mental turmoil, and would certainly do no harm.

There were no familiar faces among the few scattered drinkers. Too early. I sat at the bar. The barman greeted me like a long lost friend and asked how the fuck was I? I foolishly told him that I was a troubled man. He laughed and said that there was obviously a serious problem with my genetic make-up, and therefore I would always be a troubled man, and there was no escaping it.

Then he asked me who was looking for me and why, just out of idle curiosity, of course. He said that he'd heard some stories. I told him to believe nobody and say nothing, especially to fat ugly red men in big black boots. He mentioned that, strangely enough, two chappies of that description had called in early the night before, but didn't stay long. They hadn't ordered any drink, as far as he could make out, and had left without speaking to anyone, as far as he could tell, but then he was busy, so he was, serving the customers and all, and he couldn't really be sure of any of the preceding information when he thought about it. In fact, it was all a bit of a blur really. Sure, it could have been the night before last – didn't they all run into each other and become one big night? He laughed again. Did I not agree?

I told him to cut the fucking fake blarney and think for a change. He laughed some more and said that was rich coming from me. I slammed my pint down, hesitated, finished it off and went out to find one of the regular doormen who would have been on duty the previous night. It took a while to get any of the fuckers to listen to me but, eventually, I got the info I didn't want to hear. The mountain men had been there the night before all right, blustery and cheeky at the door, and a bit tense-looking, and had only stayed about five minutes. The doorman asked me what all the fuss was about, and joked that I was looking a bit rough, even rougher than usual, but I just mumbled a begrudging thanks and left.

Christ, I thought the red running dogs were going to give me a week, not a day. And that was at least two of my regular bars they knew about – how many more, and where were they getting the information from? From barmen probably, like that comical gobshite I was just talking to, who would squeal on his own customers for a laugh. I looked carefully about as I walked and took the shortest route home. I packed up my personal belongings slowly and made sure nothing important was left out. The collected items didn't amount to much. I stacked them near the door and waited impatiently for McNabb to arrive.

I fidgeted and fretted and fussed as the final hour dragged by. I paced up and down the kitchen and glared intermittently at the clock, high on the wall, and then at the biscuit tin placed strategically on a shelf nearby. I worked myself into a furious tangle of guilt and denial, on top of all the other, still simmering, mental self-abuses of the day.

Five minutes before McNabb was due to appear, I took a last desperate look at the clock, its longest arm ticking away the seconds in tiny jerks. Its sound seemed totally out of proportion to its size and I realised that, over the years, I'd only noticed it when I was angry or impatient about something, and then its constant ticking noise used to annoy the shit out of me. The rest of the time, when I was feeling fine, I never even registered the fact that it was there. It seemed to summarise something about this house, the Wife, our relationship, everything. I felt like ripping it off the wall.

Instead, I pulled the lid off the biscuit tin, and helped myself to the banknotes inside. I counted them out quickly – one hundred and eighty-five quid, mostly in twenties with some fives – and stuffed them into my back pocket.

It was a nasty move. I tried hard to justify it to myself. I was going to need as much money as I could get, in case I had to do a real runner and leave the city for a while. I couldn't rely on the magazine to provide any extras now that I was sick and unavailable. I couldn't ask McNabb for money, especially after his little speech the night before. I had to take this cash. It wasn't mine, but, in the final analysis, so what? It was our house and she had kicked me out. She had all this stuff around me and I hadn't even enough to fill McNabb's car for one journey. She wouldn't really miss the money so much, I had to tell myself repeatedly, knowing I was dead wrong.

One hundred and eighty-five pounds was good. The tin usually held anything between twenty and three hundred, depending on innumerable factors. The Wife used it as a repository for all kinds of surplus notes, from extra cash still in her purse at the end of the month, or from money left over unexpectedly after a night out, or from a regular shopping trip, or a fiver here and there when she felt like it, when she had saved something on a lucky bargain, maybe, or done a bit of extra work. It was money set aside specifically for middle-range household purchases – for new furniture or fittings, an ornament or two, or something decorative to add to the glamour of our fashionable home, or a bit of fencing to spice up the garden.

Very occasionally she would have used it as a kind of ad hoc plenary indulgence box when, if she felt suitably contrite for some foolish misdeed or sinful omission, she would throw in a twenty and feel better already. There were a lot more twenties than usual, this time round. I wondered briefly what she might have been feeling guilty about. I assumed it was me. But by that stage I didn't really care. I would simply take the burden of her guilt and add it to my own. I would absolve her in the final act of my leaving and free her for a new start. It was a kind of parting agreement, on my part anyway, for the future, for our mutual benefit.

So, in one greedy grab in a biscuit tin, I made it almost impossible to renegotiate my position. I would never be back. McNabb's car pulled up, right on time. I knew, as I silently and morosely ferried out my meagre possessions, that I would never sleep under this roof again. Fuck it.

McNabb said nothing as we drove off. He had sensed my mood immediately on arriving and kept the exchange of words to a minimum. It didn't stop him looking intently in my direction every now and again, though, but I couldn't return his gaze.

mex's place [3]

I woke up on the settee with a sore head, sore guts, sore shins, sore finger, sore mouth, and, much to my alarm, a sore cock. I had to think about where I was for a second or two. Then I noticed the yellow and black tartan blanket on the floor beside me. I looked at my watch in the dim, half-formed light and groaned loudly to alert anyone in the vicinity that I was alive and about to move. It was late in the morning and the curtains had been pulled apart just enough to let in a thin chink of sunshine, a fine line of brightness running along the floor and touching the wall just within my field of vision as I sat up. Sunshine? Despite my condition, I forced myself to stand up and to move slowly and painfully towards the light. I hadn't seen any sunshine for about two months.

I whipped open the curtains and was instantly transported to another country, another climate, another life. The sun dazzled and toasted me as I stood dazed and glued to the floor. My eyes grew quickly accustomed to the glare and they feasted on the brilliant blue of the sky and the vibrant shapes of the street below, shimmering and glowing in sharp contrasts of colour and tone. I breathed in deeply, painfully – sore ribs as well, bejesus – and let out a long, loud sigh. I felt sick, annoyed, apprehensive, scared, wrecked, hopeful, elated, and kind of happy, all at the same time.

I turned around slowly to survey the state of things in what could be my new abode for a while – depending on circumstances, of course, I wouldn't let myself get too optimistic – and I was shocked by two things. First, the sunlight disappeared almost immediately behind me and, second, an empty vodka bottle stood on the work surface of the kitchen with a sheet of paper, a note of some sort, underneath it. Had I really drunk a full bottle of vodka? I didn't even like the fucking stuff. I turned back to see what had happened to the sun, and the sudden sight and sound of raindrops hit me like a punch to the kidneys. Dark clouds had appeared across the top of the window and were moving in fast. It was a Saturday, last week in June, almost midday, and I had snored through the only fleeting sign of summer given to us since last year. Strange, sad, murky emotions welled up in me, and a deathly feeling overcame me as if my liver had just collapsed. I longed for the sun to come back, with a longing I'd rarely experienced before – a graveside longing, a deeply resonant regret that knew no limits.

I was a kid again, trying not to cry, as I went over to the note, fearing the worst. It was a relief to discover a handwritten, factual message to the effect that Mex had to go to her studio in town, that she was sorry but would be back around two o'clock, that I should wait for her and make myself at home. I didn't think about it. I had to wait. But it didn't take long for the thinking to start.

No mention of Matt in the note, thank Christ, or maybe that wasn't a good thing, maybe she was hiding something. She said that she was expecting him today. What for? Maybe he wasn't her boyfriend at all. Then who was he? Why hadn't I asked her when I had the chance? Regrets, questions and regrets, and rain and more rain. Neurotic expectations and bad connections. How do we keep going sometimes? Rain, rain, go to Spain. Sunshine, sunshine, come again. My mama told me there'd be days like this. No, she fucking didn't. Sunshine on a rainy day. Stupid songs going round in my head. Songs and faded memories jumping around in a swamp of mixed-up emotions. I was cracking up for sure. I had to go and do something, clean myself up.

I went looking for aspirins and swallowed six. I stood in the shower for about twenty minutes, trying to wash away my various aches and pains and dopy songs. It seemed to work. I searched for a fresh blade for the razor I'd seen among the lotions the previous night, and wondered about my logic, or lack of it, to be more precise. I just very

recently had had unprotected sex with someone I knew
nothing about, and there I was looking for a new blade to
protect myself from possible contamination by a razor that
looked like it had never been used. I found some blades
and a neat little foam spray – she took care of small things,
this girl – and shaved carefully to a clean, pinkish finish. I
added the worry of unprotected sex and its possible
consequences to my long list of problems and it sank into
the swamp without a trace. Number one problem was
Matt the Wanker. Number two was how to sufficiently
impress Mex, so that I might be able to stay for a while.
The rest could wait. Clear thoughts. That was more like it.
I rubbed myself vigorously with the towel.

I wandered into her bedroom and looked around. It was
pretty much like the front room – low, tidy furniture,
neatly arranged, not much clutter, just a few clothes and
some books lying near the bed. I rummaged through a
stack of T-shirts in the wardrobe and selected a large black
one with 'Numero Uno' printed across it in white letters.
Perfect. I even found a pair of newish boxer shorts that
fitted me. I hated boxer shorts – somehow they always
managed to get caught up around my balls – but it was
either them or a pair of tight, girlie knickers, which might
have been fun, but not in the present circumstances. There
were quite a few pairs of boxers, folded nicely into a
wardrobe compartment with some nightie-type things. I
guessed that they were part of Mex's night-time attire on
occasions. I imagined her walking about in them. As soon
as I pulled them on I could feel warm stirrings in their
interior.

Within a short space of time I was seated cleanly and

respectably in the kitchen area, sipping a coffee. Externally, I was shiny and presentable. I was the picture of relaxed, casual, early Saturday readiness for the weekend ahead. I even found some amazing American eye drops, to banish, almost completely, the shocking red blaze from around my eyeballs.

Internally, my physical ailments, especially the wrenched, corkscrewed gut and the jangling nerves, were just about bearable. My bubbling mental stew had reduced itself to a simmer, only erupting now and again with a sudden nagging question or spurt of self-consciousness and doubt. I needed something to do, some mental distraction, nothing too intellectual. I didn't like the look of Mex's books. I was also dubious about her CD collection. Girlie stuff probably, I figured, all the usual Annies and Marys and Jonis and Bjorks. I rifled roughly through the discs stacked beside the hi-fi system. I was wrong. I found *Bitches Brew*, one of my old favourite Miles Davis sets, near the top of the pile. It didn't seem like the sort of music Mex would be interested in somehow, but, then again, she was full of surprises, a real groovy, eclectic, ethnic chic kind of a gal. I slid the disc into the mini-player, and turned it up to a healthy volume.

The required mental state for effective seduction, or battle, or both, is, as it always has been, a state of detached equanimity. I knew it then, in theory, as well as I know it now, but I also knew that I could never achieve it. I was prepared to settle for nervous and excited, and a bit frazzled, but, on the surface, cool. Cool and poised for action. Good old Miles, bless his soul, and his bad buddies clunking away and playing loud and free, were just the ticket for my psychic preparation.

Then I waited. I lay down on the settee, sat up, paced about, lay down. The biggest effort, at this point, was restraining myself from going into the small study and looking at any more photographs. I'd already checked the Bill and Ben Polaroid, just to be sure I hadn't been hallucinating or suffering from paranoid delusions, and at the sight of it, something had pulled at my stomach. So I'd quickly pinned it back into its rightful place and left the room. I was in no condition to explore any further, but I was still curious about Mex's friends and connections.

I paced about some more. I put on the second CD of the set as soon as the first had finished. It was cool all right, energising, uplifting, like a favourite mantra gone into overdrive – a series of syncopated grooves, as we used to say in the business, way out there, unpredictable, bent, tangential, the kind that lift you up and carry you along with them. I hopped and jigged a bit and paced about. I was getting impatient for something to happen, anything. There was beer in the fridge, but I was resisting.

I busied myself with rearranging the CD collection into order of musical importance, with Miles at the top and Sandie Shaw at the bottom. I thought Mex might like that, and it made some kind of statement about our shared musical tastes. Then I arranged it again with the Wu-Tang Clan at the bottom, in case she got annoyed about the sexist overtones of the first choice. Then I spotted Garth Brooks. How come I missed him? He was going straight to the bottom when a buzzer rang somewhere near the hallway door.

I rushed to find it. Right beside the door there was a

small metal intercom box with two plastic buttons on it. I pushed at the grey button. I didn't know whether I should say anything. It might be him or someone else, not her. The chrome box screeched a bit, and then emitted a hum and a crackle of distant, broken words.

'Hello? It's Matt. Open the door. Can you hear me?'

I pushed the green button and heard the loud metallic buzz as the lock on the front door released its catch. Then I could make out heavy footsteps on the stairs. I opened the hall door and stepped back into the main room. I turned the music down just a bit, not too much, and stood facing the door. I wanted to intimidate him but I also wanted to hear what he had to say for himself, if anything. Me and Miles, running the voodoo down. Myles and Miles, we had the advantage, the element of surprise.

Like fuck we had. I nearly collapsed when I saw him. He stepped into the room and I practically had to gasp for air. He glanced at me briefly, with no sign of surprise or indignation or anything, and took a quick look around the room, then back at me again. This was too much, too unbelievable, too weird.

It's impossible for me now to describe adequately the mixed feelings and sensations that charged through me at that moment. Miles's trumpet soared and dipped, and shook me to the core as I lost hold of something inside. Something central, deeply familiar, slipped and was gone. No, not something, everything. Everything was lost, all the shit and all the sunshine.

My sense of myself and my own identity evaporated for an instant and I was pure sound, pure consciousness of sound, a soaring and tumbling of sound, and pure sight, the kind of sharp, bright sight that comes with raw surprise. I was standing there looking at myself. For a long, long, long few seconds.

It was me. He was me, only a few years younger, with slightly shorter hair, wet with the rain. He was even dressed like me, with a black T-shirt, minus the logo, and blue jeans, and a black leather jacket that looked like my beat-up old thing, except thinner and lighter and more stylish-looking. A lot of trendy fuckers dressed like that, like me, like I'd always done. But it was the face, my face, that was impossible.

'She's not here, is she? You must be Myles. You look a bit shocked,' he said, loudly but calmly.

'How did you know?' was all I could say. Of course I looked shocked. I was worse than shocked. It had been one of my worst fears, as a child, to go to bed and find myself already in there, in the bed, fast asleep. My mother used to tell me to shut up about it, to stop imagining things and to give her head peace. Her impatient, vicious looks used to tear me apart. A flash of deep, remembered childhood pain gripped me momentarily, a feeling of something heavy expanding away from me, a feeling of empty space. I was slipping again. Something strange was beginning to open up in my head, much deeper and darker than the swamp – a black hole of repressed associations, nasty memories. I really was cracking up. I was going insane, in front of myself. The drift was halted in time by the sound of Matt's raised voice.

'Can I turn that racket down?'

He must have said it a couple of times before I noticed. He gestured impatiently towards the hi-fi and then moved over in a shuffling, smiling, sideways fashion to lower the volume. He turned it right down low, too low for someone just arrived in somebody else's space. Then he started talking.

'How did I know your name? She told me last night, on the phone. She phoned me from that hotel near here, round the corner, what's it called?'

'Nooks,' I said. An automatic response. She phoned from the bar? What was he talking about? Wait a minute. Something clicked. On one of her trips to the toilet, earlier on, she took a hell of a long time. What the fuck was going on?

'Yeah. That's it. Nooks.' He was relaxed, just imparting information, no more, no less. 'She phoned me from there, and asked me to come down as soon as possible to see her, to meet you. She said it was for her work, and it was important. So here I am. I drove down from Derry as soon as I could, like I told her. Rain most of the way and then driving round in circles looking for a parking space and she's not even here. Typical. I'm Matt, by the way. Did she not tell you what she was at?'

He grinned in a condescending sort of way, and stuck out his hand. I shook it, and a curious sensation ran through me. I cleared my throat, and spoke slowly, carefully.

'She told me you might call in today. But she didn't say much about it. What's going on? What did she mean, her work?'

He sat down on the settee, took some cigarettes from his coat pocket, and pointed the box at me. I shook my head. He lit up and blew some smoke sideways towards the CD player. 'Any beer in the fridge? Can I have one?' he said.

I was glad he mentioned the beer, as I was already moving towards the kitchen.

'I don't really know what's going on,' he continued.

I pulled two bottles from the fridge, opened them quickly, took a long, cool slurp from mine, and handed him the other one over the work surface. He had to lean over hard to reach it, and I was hoping that he'd rip the seam of his fancy coat.

'All I know is that she asked me to come down here. She wants to take some photographs. Of us, me and you. She didn't even ask you about it?' He smiled and shook his head slightly. 'She's always in a hurry. She has a big show coming up soon and she always gets up to high doh before an exhibition. She's fucking nuts sometimes. But, you only just met her, right . . . last night? Anyway, she obviously thinks we look alike, and she wants to use us for her show . . .'

Was he blind? Was he stupid? Of course we looked alike. Like twins, or brothers, more like – he definitely looked younger, about six or seven years, maybe, now that I could see him better. It was still fucking scary, though, and he didn't even seem to notice. He was happy to talk away, giving information, drinking and smoking, enjoying a relaxed Saturday afternoon, a little chat between new buddies, easy-going, just passing the time, the wanker. I had to admit to myself, though, reluctantly, that his manner and voice, and the taste of beer, and the music, quieter now in the background, were all calming me down a little. But where was that conniving little bitch? I let him talk.

'She's into this doppelgänger thing these days. I think she exhausted the twin market a while back and decided to look for doubles instead. Wouldn't surprise me if she was going to use us along with some other pairs of lookalikes, to fake some extra photos. She'll want to pose us as twins to complete the series or something like that, to fill the gaps. She's like that. She's a laugh, but she's nuts. Sometimes I think she'll do anything to push her career as an artist. When I met her, she was taking photographs of everyone she knew . . .'

My sickness and confusion and bad nerves were beginning to coalesce and transform themselves into a tiny ball of anger, as the dickhead from Derry talked on. I really had taken a liking to that sneaky bitch and it looked like she had set me up, just to get a fucking photograph. She had let me screw her and taken me back here, so that she could arrange this fool to arrive as soon as possible, to use the two of us as mugs for her art, her profession, for the aesthetic benefit of all, no doubt.

I could feel myself getting riled up and I was surprised how good it felt. Meanwhile, Matt the Moron was chatting on, regardless of whether I was listening or not. I noticed something similar on my enforced visits to Derry for gigs and festivals. Everybody talked a lot and nobody listened. And everybody was unnaturally and unconditionally cheerful – the happy chatterboxes from the windy city, all talking their way out of what? They had the highest suicide rate in Ireland, and a twenty-four-hour watch on the River Foyle in winter to prevent the rate increasing, or so I'd been told. They also thought Belfast people were cynical bastards. They were right. And Mex was a Belfast girl through and through, by the look of things.

'. . . and then I met her again in Derry when she was doing a show there. I helped her to build some stuff for the installation thing she was doing, you know, a video projection with big wooden structures and mirrors. I couldn't make much sense of it myself, but the gallery paid me well for the work. I said that I would return the favour sometime. So here I am. I'm not very busy, but I wish she had given me a bit more notice. I don't really like coming down to Belfast unless I have to. I don't like the bars here – nobody ever talks about anything, they just stand around in groups and get drunk and make noise, like a bunch of fucking penguins. Are you from here?'

I shuddered and then nodded. 'Yeah. Want another beer?'

'That was quick. No thanks. I've some left here. I don't drink that fast. I was wondering if she would get in contact again. The last time I saw her was only a few months ago . . .'

I got a beer for myself. Well, at least one thing was clear – I wouldn't have to drag any information out of him. And some other things were becoming clearer by the minute. Mex was a fake, that was for sure. I'd thought, maybe, for once, for a change, that something good was happening to me, but she was just using me as a patsy, for a fucking arty photograph that meant nothing to me or to her other patsy. He owed her a favour, that's all, but I owed her nothing. The poor bastard obviously didn't care about being used. He was happy as long as he could chitter away to somebody, or something – his beer bottle would do, for Christ's sake, in place of me.

It was also obvious that he wasn't her boyfriend. They might have had something going in Derry for a while, but I doubted it, the way he was talking about her. He didn't seem her type anyway. Too innocent. It was also beginning to look like the mountain men were merely part of her twins project. She probably didn't know anything useful about them, useful for me, that was. I could feel some questions dissolving and disappearing from the swamp, leaving a bit of room for mental reorientation. I was thankful for that, but there were other things to be taken care of. First, I had to talk to Mex, alone, as soon as she came back, and see what she had to say for herself. Then, depending on her story, I would either get the hell out of there, or else stay a while, get rid of Matt, relax, drink her beer and see what happened. There was always the hope that she was more than just a pushy, fucked-up arty spook. I wanted to find that out. I couldn't help my feelings towards her, even if they made no sense at all.

Then I would have to phone the Wife and find out what she was doing in Nooks. There was something not right about that – she rarely went out drinking any more, except with her family, and they only drank in their local pubs. If I could get her to talk to me, and not scream or ask too many questions, she might also be able to tell me if the cops were called to investigate the circumstances of the bouncer's sore jaw. Everything depended on whether or not she had looked in her biscuit tin within the last few days – if not, I might be able to get some information, otherwise I could expect a stream of dog's abuse and not much else. The main problem was that McNabb would go crazy, well maybe not crazy, but he would have to reconsider the situation, if he found out that the RUC were looking for me as well as the red fuckers. I thought I'd better phone him too, to let him know that I was all right, and to see if he had any good news for me, in terms of whatever he was up to behind the scenes. But I had to talk to Mex first – maybe, just maybe, we could work something out and I could lie low in her place for a while and forget about everything else.

Christ, my weekend was turning into a real social whirl. I was working myself into a terrible tizzy, trying to juggle my commitments. Matt was still enjoying himself, smoking and talking away, mostly about Derry and the local football team and their bad season. I nodded to him every now and again, and watched how his face moved as he spoke. He smiled a lot to himself and pulled forcefully on his cigarettes. He raised his right eyebrow a bit when he anticipated a nod, making things easier for me.

I helped myself to another beer. I was satisfied that he was an idiot, harmless, but I could see why people might like him. He was comfortable with himself and he had a very relaxed manner. I began to think of him less as a wanker and more as a kind of apprentice Lad, a bit like myself, apart from the incessant rabbiting. He was a nuisance at the moment, though, just by being there, but I no longer considered him a threat to any possible relationship I may or may not pursue with the ruthless Mex.

Where the fuck was she? I drank at my beer impatiently and leaned over a few times from my seat near the window to look out at the street below, as if it would hasten her arrival somehow. Matt told me affably, like a good friend, to relax, that she was always late. The music had stopped and he began searching through the CDs while I looked at the rain, easing off now just a bit. Maybe the sun would appear again and I could sit quietly in its glare with my eyes closed, and feel the warmth and colour seep into me. Matt put on some good old rock music, as I knew he would, early R.E.M., which I quite liked, so I said nothing. But then he turned it up a few notches, smiled over at me, and turned it up louder again. He did a little dance movement, a kind of shake and shuffle in time with the music, as he went to get another beer from the fridge. I scowled at him but he didn't even notice. It was the usual fucking story – give them an inch, relax with them for two minutes, and what happens? They take over.

I went out to the bathroom to get away from the noise. I pushed the door closed, hard, and stood in front of the mirror for a long time, under the fluorescent wall light, trying to imagine it was the sun on my face. I looked at myself closely. I thought about the wanker's face and how it was different from mine. There wasn't a lot I could actually pinpoint, apart from the less puffy eyes and the slightly narrower shape. I was making allowance for the various furrows and creases of my extra years, of course, because they weren't the essential face, the essence of the looks, the prime matter. That was the same in both cases. Maybe his eyes were darker, but I couldn't make out their colour from the distance we had been maintaining from each other. I was still amazed that he didn't see anything extraordinary in the coincidence. He was completely blasé about it, the fucking idiot. Maybe Mex's phone call had prepared him sufficiently for the encounter, and so, for him, patsy or no patsy, it was just a favour to be returned, just business.

Then I looked at myself, as myself alone, for a while. I breathed deeply. I appeared reasonably calm and collected, and pretty sharp for a thirty-nine-year-old drunk undergoing severe mental and physical traumas, inflicted on me by assholes and wankers. My current physical ailments had settled into a kind of dull uncomfortable droning sensation in the general background of my awareness – something I was well used to. The drone would continue until enough drink was consumed to block it out altogether. But I looked OK. And I felt much better about my position with Mex. I was going to let her have it, for sure; give her a good talking to when she came back, put her on the spot properly, and find out what was really going on. I had to be careful, though, not too aggressive, not too hasty about breaking off any possibilities for the future. Always keep your options open, Myles, my old mate, that was the way to handle it. When I had reassured myself sufficiently, I decided to go back to the front room and assert myself. I was going to turn the music down, sit at the window quietly, and wait.

I returned to the main room. The hall door to the stairs was open and there was no sign of Matt. Probably gone to get cigarettes, or something. Good. I didn't want to hear any more crap about the Derry football team and their missed opportunities. I turned the volume down to a reasonable level on the CD player, lifted my beer, and sat at the window. I waited for the sun, or Mex, or both, to arrive before that idiot got back. That would be a good sign. I would be happy enough with that. I sang along with the music a little. I was thinking positive.

mcnabb's place [2]

McNabb reversed the car carefully and parked right next to the step of his big front door, well hidden from human sight by walls, trees and bushes. We had hardly spoken during the short journey, and now I was getting annoyed at him for being so conspicuously careful. There was no real justification for the vague resentment I was feeling towards him. He was just being cautious, looking after both our interests. He didn't have to do this, after all. He was doing me a big favour and I was getting angrier and more irritated by the minute.

There was something wrong about his manner. His over-carefulness seemed strange to me, too calculated, paranoid even. His protective behaviour was just a bit too pronounced. It was annoying me all right – I was the one in trouble here, not him. What was he so worried about? Not that he looked particularly worried. He looked like he always looked, distant and attentive at the same time, preoccupied but aware.

He busied himself upstairs as I unloaded my precious possessions – the bulk of my CD and tape collection in some boxes, my chunky little sound system, bags of clothes, boots, a few personal effects, a small case of documents, and some books and magazines, that was it. I sank down into one of his spongy chairs and stared aggressively at the summary of my life history to date. He reappeared after a while, sat down opposite me, and took a long silent look at the pile of scruffy cardboard boxes, beat-up bags, and bumpy black bin-liners stacked carelessly in the middle of his neat living-room floor. I half expected him to say something witty and humorous and a bit coy, just to break the tension, but McNabb was McNabb, good-natured and clear-sighted, even under pressure.

'I'll give you the money,' he said, still looking at the angular, ugly mound.

'Down-sizing is becoming fashionable in Ireland,' I replied after a while. 'Did you know that?'

He smiled and looked out the window. I could feel my anger dissolving into guilt, or shame, or something similar that made me squirm a little inside.

'If you want it,' he added after a long pause.

'No. No. You were right. I need to sort this out myself. All of it. It's not just the money. It's the whole mess. I'll phone Bigelow and see if he'll give me some more time. I could probably get work with one of the local newspapers and try to get enough money together to pay him off gradually. I'll check it out as soon as possible, and we'll see what happens.'

I surprised myself. Who was this noble, upright person, suddenly mature and responsible, taking control of the situation? Why didn't I just take the money and save everybody a whole lot of unnecessary pain, especially me? Was I stubborn or stupid or both? Or too proud? What the fuck was wrong with me? I was just about to renege on my newly found principles when McNabb rose and moved towards the door.

'All right,' he said. 'I'm glad. It's better that way, but don't phone Bigelow from here. Use a phone box. I have to go. Here's a key for the front door. By the way, there's whiskey in the cupboard. Leave me some.'

He chuckled to himself, discreetly, of course, threw me the key, and left for work again.

Clear-sighted was right. Clear-fucking-sighted was a pain in the ass. I was angry again. I wasn't going to use the fucking phone, anyway. I knew that sitting there, feeling angry and stupid, and staring at my bumpy pile on the floor wasn't going to get me very far on the road to recovery, so I went to the kitchen. I had a quick whiskey. Then I carted the offending articles upstairs to my room and piled them up there instead.

I couldn't help thinking about McNabb's work. There must be a reason for his constant guarded behaviour and his over-diligent watchfulness. Apart from the obvious one, that was, of not wanting a demented, screaming wife on his front doorstep, closely followed by two sullen fat men with baseball bats, or knives, or whatever their favourite weapons of punishment happened to be. The top secret stuff he so carefully avoided talking about must be pretty important. I wondered who his associates were negotiating with – politicians, obviously, but maybe also paramilitaries, the RUC the Brits, MI5, the whole scary bunch, who knows? Even the dumbest dogs knew that all the really important deals in this forsaken little statelet were done behind the scenes, during secret meetings in the strangest locations.

Maybe McNabb was one of the real engineers of our future, peace or no peace, carefully and meticulously cultivating something new, with his well-trained team of discrepancy-spotters and opinion-monitors beavering away in sparsely furnished boardrooms, while the politicians strutted and pranced about for the media outside. It wouldn't have surprised me at all. Come to think of it, he had gradually developed, over the years, that kind of seasoned statesman-like air about him. He had the faintly sanctimonious look of a man who knew what was really going on in the belly of the beast but refused to talk about it for the public good.

This was probably the worst time for me to be around him, getting under his feet, dragging him into my pathetic shambles of a life. He had been more than gracious about the whole unsavoury business. And what did I do? I got angry and sulky with him because he parked his car as close to the door as possible, so that no one would see my rubbish going into his house. So that I wouldn't have to carry my decrepit belongings too far, was more the truth of the matter.

I couldn't be left on my own for ten minutes. I was tearing myself to pieces. I needed more than money, I needed some serious help. Did I know any psychiatrists, who would take me on at short notice? I started to play mockingly with the the idea of knocking on the door of some institution and asking to be taken in. That would be a real laugh. There had to be an alternative. There always was. I thought for a while. Benny the barman, in the Green Room, was a good amateur shrink, a good listener, and a giver of age-old wisdom and advice, even if most of it was a load of chickenshit. And some of my old mates might be there at this time of the afternoon. If ever I needed some easy company, it was now. What about the mountain men, I thought. They couldn't possibly know about the Green Room. I hardly ever went there. And I had to make that phone call to Bigelow from somewhere. So, off I went to the Green Room, just like that.

Benny wasn't there when I arrived. It was probably his day off. There was no one around I could talk to. I nodded casually to some of the regulars and old hands, who always shuffled in and out to the bookies next door at regular intervals, but they were no good to me today. All they talked about was horses and bets, and they never listened to anything, not even hot tips. Just my luck. I ordered a pint and braced myself for the phone call I had to make. I downed the drink quickly and ordered another one. I carried it carefully over to the public phone.

I pulled a stool over and set a stack of coins on the shelf

above. I was getting ready for a long and convoluted conversation, where I would more or less disgrace myself as a human being by begging for time to pay off my lousy debts.

As chance would have it, Bigelow was in his office, primed and ready, or so it seemed, to receive my call. He laughed as soon as I identified myself. The sound of his faked, drawn-out, soap-opera laugh made me involuntarily push my pint away from the phone, as if it would be contaminated somehow.

'Ah, it's you, my old son,' he said eventually. 'I've been expecting a call from you. I suppose you want to come to some arrangement about the fucking dosh you owe me. Just like that, eh? At your fucking convenience, now that you've had a little fright.'

I tried to answer, but he talked on, excited as hell.

'Well, business is business, but I'll tell you something for nothing, you fucking little sod, with you I'm going to make an exception. I heard one of your local paddy sayings the other day, a really nice little number – "you sicken my shite". Well, you fucking sicken my shite, you little cunt, with your fucking phone calls and cheeky letters, and I'm going to have you, as an example to some of your friends. I'm going to have you. Forget the money. I want you, and my boys want you. They've taken a strong dislike to you, and I can see why, and they can't wait to get their big fucking clumsy hands on your balls. So, I've given them the go-ahead to kick the living shit out of you, you little prick. I told them to take their time and give you a good working over. How do you like that, you fucking little . . .'

I hung up, and threw up at the same time, away from my pint and onto the floor. One of the old-timers near the phone said loudly to his fellow betting men, sitting on solitary stools around the bar, like they always did, that my horse had come last. They all laughed and coughed out cigarette smoke.

'And his girlfriend's pregnant,' one of them added, and they all laughed again.

'And the baby's black,' said another, to more raucous cackles and coughs.

I just sat there, stranded in my own vomit.

Benny's replacement wasn't too pleased about the mess. I could tell by his wrinkly face. He came over slowly with an old-fashioned bucket and mop and started to clean around me. I didn't really know him, but he asked me if I was all right. I nodded, thankful for any little sympathy. He looked at me closely. Then he asked me if I was the fellow who wrote the what's-on column in the entertainment magazine that Benny sometimes kept in the bar for the customers. I nodded again, wiping my mouth, and shaking a bit at the outer extremities. I hadn't thrown up for about fifteen years.

Then he told me the bad news, with a hint of malice forced into the slow annunciation of the details, to get his own back for the cleaning job, I assumed. Two big fellows with red hair had called in just about an hour ago asking about me. They had a copy of the magazine, with the tiny black-and-white photograph at the top of my column. It wasn't a good likeness, he said. It must have been an old magazine because I looked a lot younger in the image. I stared at the wet floor and noticed the tiny streaks of coloured bile in the dark stain where he had mopped up. It had never even crossed my mind that some of those old copies would still be around somewhere.

I said that he was right, that we had stopped using photographs of the writers and columnists a while back because we were fed up getting harassed in pubs. I asked him what he had told the red buggers. Nothing. He was only Benny's stand-in. What the frig did he know about anything? And, besides, he didn't like the look of them. He said they looked like the sort of fellows who would do you over for tuppence, and who wouldn't let up very easily. They looked like frigging UVF men or something, murderers once and will be again if these ceasefires didn't hold, and I'd better watch out. He said that they were probably still driving around right now, from pub to pub looking for me, and that I should go home the long way round.

I asked him for another pint, and he said I should leave, that he didn't want any trouble. I slouched towards the door, and one of the old punters waved and laughed and shouted to take it easy, Myles. Christ Almighty, who was he, and how did he know me? And how many people around this city knew me from that stupid photograph? Or from bar-room episodes that I couldn't even remember? Or from joke-telling sessions and drunken singsongs also long forgotten? Or binges and parties nearly every night for years on end, before the Wife started to put the foot down? The fact of my relatively high profile existence hadn't registered with me until now. And there I was in the Green Room, making sure everybody noticed me even more. I realised that nearly every barman in town was probably curious now about my day-to-day business, after years of watching me come and go. I looked about cautiously as I left and spat the sour taste of vomit from my mouth.

I called into a pub down the road, a noisy, sporty kind of joint that I would never drink in, and sat for ages over a couple of bad pints, gazing blankly at the main door from a far-distant corner seat. Some young spicy girls giggled and moved away from me when I sat down. A year or two ago, they would have been chatting away to me within five minutes. It was different now – not the same Myles any more. No more reckless charm or saucy banter or openness or just drunken good humour. I'd lost it, whatever it was, probably for good. I was a loser. I was a fucking loser all right.

mex's place [4]

The R.E.M. songs had finished on a positive note. I was content to leave it like that, so I didn't move. I slumped further into Mex's chair. I was half-dozing, watching a little blue patch in the sky through the rain-streaked window, when I heard a sudden loud commotion in the front hall, down below. The door to the apartment was still ajar – and I could hear the clatter and bang of something heavy being dumped on the hall floor down-stairs, and then another, sort of metallic, clump, followed by scraping noises and dull thuds. I jumped up and looked out the window at the pathway below. No sign of anyone – nothing except parked cars along the street. My heart started to race. I didn't know what to do. I looked around frantically for something to use as a weapon, just in case my worst fears were confirmed. If the red bastards had somehow tracked me down, I wasn't just going to say hello to them and follow them out to their waiting car to be taken away and beaten to a pulp, was I? No way. Not now. I grabbed the designer lamp and held it upside down, so that the base became a deadly weapon.

I heard slow, heavy footsteps and a huffing and puffing on the stairs, and more scraping noises against the walls. I moved to the centre of the room and braced myself for the confrontation. I couldn't get a proper grip on the lamp – it was unbalanced and unwieldy, no matter what way I held it. Fucking useless designers. The noises got closer. I started to sweat. I steadied myself. The door was kicked fully open, and I got set to charge. Here we go. Here we fucking go. I was ready for hell. There was a flurry of movement and Mex staggered into the room, with angular metal arms and legs sticking out of her all over the place. She dumped a large tripod roughly onto the floor, followed by two spotlights with some kind of shiny stands, and what looked like a camera bag, with bits and pieces protruding from its cover. She was pink-faced and gasping for air and soaked to the skin through a light summer jacket and jeans. She stared at me, wide-eyed. She looked gorgeous.

'I couldn't get a taxi,' she blurted. Then she burst out laughing. 'What are you doing?'

I lowered the lamp, and set it carefully on the floor. I tried to look as unembarrassed as possible by freezing into a rigid upright stance, expressionless, unblinking, ridiculous.

'Numero Uno,' she said, laughing again. 'That's my favourite T-shirt.'

I stood stock still, unable to move. Then a stir. The light changed dramatically for a moment or two, brightened a bit, wavered on the edge of some kind of flux, and then flooded into a section of the bay window in a burst of colour and warmth. The rest of the room lit up simultaneously, and everything blazed with importance. Mex looked even more gorgeous.

I started to cry. Out of shame, out of embarrassment, out of tiredness and exhaustion, out of resentment and self-pity, out of confusion, out of anger, out of frustration, out of sheer joy – I really didn't know. Then the light changed again, dropped, darkened, back to normal, and I cried even more.

I was blubbering like a child, and something inside me longed for release, but there was no possibility of figuring it out. I hadn't cried since I was about twelve, apart from a few hidden tearlets during the odd Lassie movie or Jackson Browne song. I just stood in the middle of the room and let it happen. I didn't give a shit any more about who might judge me or what might happen to me, I just wanted to let everything drop, let everything go, and feel the real tears on my face, and sob, and be who I was once, sometime long ago, before I became what I was now.

Mex came close to me and draped her arms loosely over my shoulders. She let me sob for a while and said nothing, until I raised my hands to wipe the wet trails from my face.

'It's your wife, isn't it?' she said slowly. 'You miss her?'

I didn't look at her. I kept my eyes to the floor. 'No. I told you, we're separated. We're finished. I want you.'

I couldn't believe the last three words I'd just let slip from my wet and salty lips. I had actually come out and said something that I really felt, without analysing it, or weighing up the possible consequences, or anticipating the next move, without any trace of irony, or sarcasm, or affectation.

'OK' was all she said, in a fashion I was getting used to, and she took me by the hand.

She led me into the bedroom, pushing the hall door closed as she passed, and proceeded to give me what the Lads would call a sympathy fuck. It was one of the most pleasurable and gratifying love-making experiences of my entire life, offered with an unfettered generosity and a unique gracefulness. And I cried most of the way through it, inwardly, silently.

Without saying a word, Mex sat me on the bed, pulled off my boots and socks, lifted my legs onto the duvet and removed my jeans effortlessly and efficiently. She smiled when she saw the familiar boxer shorts, and simply reached in and pulled my cock gently out of the central slit. She let it rest sideways on the fabric of the shorts at an approximate three o'clock position, from her vantage point. She then stood and removed her clothes slowly and carefully, with a confident, encouraging smile on her face, all the time watching my cock as it grew thicker and longer and started to swivel around towards twelve o'clock. By the time she leaned over to kiss it, it was extended and hard, and, at the touch of her lips, it jerked itself involuntarily into perfect line at high noon.

I couldn't see her face properly, as it was tilted downwards, but I could tell she was amused as she slipped her mouth over the gleaming tip and started to move her head slowly up and down. I was still kind of crying, still silently, my eyes now shut, and my mind blanked out by the intense feeling in my groin as she applied her skills. I only opened my eyes some minutes later, when she let my cock pop from her mouth. She slid her body upwards and forwards to manoeuvre her belly on top of mine. I watched as she moved backwards again softly to take the hot stiffness into her, wet into wetness, a fluid, frictionless penetration. The boxer shorts tightened perfectly around my balls, a world apart from the usual chafing tangle, intensifying the pleasure incredibly, and I stopped crying and began to moan.

Mex just worked away quietly, slim and soft, cool and efficient, doing very little except rocking up and down almost imperceptibly. She gave her breasts a little shake to encourage me to hold them. And then she came, easily, calmly, groaning deeply and pursing her lips. And then I came, with a stretched, taut mouth making a low sound, echoing her groans, and sunlight bursting behind my eyelids.

We lay back for a long time and said nothing. Then she got up and went to the bathroom. She looked good as she moved, straight-backed and elegant. She returned shortly and lifted down a long, white dressing gown from a hook behind the door, and then disappeared again. I was sitting on the bed thinking about getting a beer when she cruised back into the room. She kissed me on the forehead and asked if I was all right. I nodded yes. Then she showed me something she was holding, and pulled us both back into the sludge of reality, not abruptly or stridently, but sharply enough to make me cringe.

'Do you know where Matt went? He was here, wasn't he? I could smell the cigarette smoke, and he always plays this.' She flipped open the empty CD cover, in a relaxed, non-accusing, curious gesture.

'I don't know where he went,' I said. 'I think he must have gone out for cigarettes or something. I was in the bathroom when he left.'

'Did you say anything to him?' She smiled a wry, concerned kind of smile. 'Did you have a row, or something? He's not my boyfriend, you know.'

I was grateful for the information. I tried to smile back at her.

'No, we didn't have a row. We were getting on like a house on fire, guzzling your beer and shooting the breeze, just like boys do on a Saturday afternoon when they've nothing better to do. No problem. Everything was hunky-dory.'

She looked at me, strangely. She probably expected me to say something about the uncanny resemblance, but I didn't want to think about it. Or maybe she just wasn't used to this old-fashioned kind of talk. Maybe I should have said something less emphatic, a bit more laid-back, more modern. Young women like their men to use the accepted parlance of the day, I reminded myself. I could recognise my thinking patterns getting back to normal.

'I tried to phone him on his mobile just now, and there was no answer. He always keeps it with him and he always keeps it on,' she said slowly.

She looked genuinely worried, and my brain moved up a gear. Was she thinking about her photographs?

'Where's the nearest place to get cigarettes?' I asked.

'Well, there's a shop at the bottom of the street. Or Nooks, it's probably closer.'

'Shit,' I hissed.

'What? Oh, right. The doorman might be there. It's OK, Matt could talk his way out of anything. And you don't look that similar. I was planning to do a bit of a make-up job on you both to get the likeness right.' She suddenly looked sheepish. 'I suppose he told you all about it, the twin thing and all, and the photo project I'm working on. I was trying to tell you . . .'

Not that similar? Was she fucking nuts? I stopped listening. And it wasn't the doorman I was thinking about. The fat men would be on the prowl with a vengeance today after what happened in the Flatfield last night. I started ranting.

'Listen. Anybody would get us mixed up. Especially in low light, in the rain, with his hair wet. He looks just like me, only younger, but you would have to look close to realise that, and you would have to know me to tell the difference, not just see me twice, both times in bars, in fucking dim light, or recognise me from a fucking stupid photograph that was taken years ago. He looks like me, he's dressed like me, he's probably gone to a bar where they must know I drink. They could be sitting outside there now or waiting in the bar. Jesus Christ, he might say the wrong thing to them, provoke the bastards. He's going to get himself fucking killed.'

She pushed her hair back on the top of her head.

'Myles, calm down. What are you talking about? The cops won't do anything to him, even if they were called. They wouldn't be round there now, anyway. They never bother with that sort of stuff, you know that as well as I do.'

The cops? How could I tell her? There wasn't enough time to explain.

'Get dressed and go round to Nooks and get him. You want to take photographs of us here, don't you? That's what all the fuss is about. That's what all the photographic gear's for, isn't it? So, let's do it, now, before the light gets worse. Go and get him now, quick. Go round to the bar and get him out of there. He must be having a couple of drinks, or he's talking to somebody. Bring him round here. No, wait. If you see two big fat guys hanging around, or in a car . . . Fuck it.'

I would have to tell her. I scrambled from the bed and hobbled into the next room, trying to straighten my boxer shorts. I pulled the Polaroid of the fat bastards off the wall again. I rushed back into the bedroom and held the photograph at her face as she tried to speak. I talked over her.

'No, listen. I haven't time to explain. If you see these two fuckers anywhere when you go out, just come back here and tell me. No, don't do that. Go to the nearest phone and phone me from there and let me know what's happening. If you see them, don't get Matt . . .'

She raised her hands to shut me up.

'How do you know those two?' she asked, indignantly, suddenly petulant. 'Some company you keep. They're really uncool, you know. I had to pay them to let me take their photograph, and then they tried to . . .'

Why wouldn't she listen?

'I know. I know. I know. Just listen. Go and get Matt, will you? Or else these two are going to beat him up, or worse. They're after me for something and they might get us mixed up. I'm fucking serious. Will you go and get him? I would do it myself, except that creepy fucker of a bouncer will probably be there, and he barred me, remember?'

Who was I kidding? I wasn't going out there. I was winding myself up for an execution, and I wasn't going anywhere until after dark.

'Those two are real bastards,' she said, 'and they're . . .'

'Yeah, I know all about them,' I said loudly. 'Now, will you go and get Matt, just in case they come snooping around there? C'mon. Hurry up!'

She hesitated, about to say something else, and then she shrugged her shoulders and started to get dressed. I pulled on my jeans and went out to have a careful, concealed look at the street from the front window. It was still raining a bit and reasonably quiet, with nobody about, the way it is on some summer Saturday afternoons. Mex left quickly through the hall door without saying anything. I shuffled over and began to close the door after her as she clicked down the stairs.

'I'll phone you from the bar,' she shouted, just before the front door banged shut. Why were there no bolts on it, or the inside door? A young woman, living here on her own, Christ, you wouldn't know what might happen.

mcnabb's place [3]

I left the sporty bar and the spicy girls to their stinking pints and their exclusive little existence, and got a taxi back to McNabb's place. Now that I had nearly two hundred pounds smouldering away in my back pocket, I could afford to play safe and use taxis to avoid the usual beaten tracks. I asked the driver to drop me at the corner of McNabb's street, and I gave him a tip for keeping his mouth shut and saying nothing during the journey.

I glanced around as I pushed back McNabb's heavy wooden side gate. Not a sinner in sight and hardly a sound to be heard, except the hushed whisper of rain-soaked trees in the wind and, far in the distance, or so it seemed, the light purr of a well-oiled engine backing into a driveway. What a charming little fucking neighbourhood. The thick foliage around and above the entrance, hiding the house almost completely from sight, splattered me with blobs of water as I banged the gate closed. I let myself in with the bright new key McNabb had given me and went straight to the kitchen, dripping rainwater all over the place.

I could hear him moving about upstairs as I poured myself a large whiskey. He came down shortly when he heard me clinking about, and greeted me in a rather cautious fashion. In fact, all he said was 'Hello Myles. Are you all right?' but there was a circumspection there, a round-aboutness, a diplomat's hesitation, that made me feel uneasy and immediately aware of the wet floor. My mother's voice somewhere in the back of my head told me I was a bloody nuisance and that I didn't care about anybody having to clean up my mess. The Wife's voice joined in. I swallowed the whiskey, and poured some more.

McNabb moved carefully across the kitchen and uncovered a plateful of food that he had cooked earlier. He told me that he had eaten already. I just stood and stared at the stuff he had prepared. Couscous or some-thing. I didn't like the look of it – it was too healthy-looking, too austere, too pallid, like something a monk would eat. He stepped around me, quickly covered the plate again and placed it in the microwave. We stood and watched as it was heated to exactly the right temperature.

I was going to tell him that he would make somebody a good wife, but I had grown weary of the W word. Instead, he took the initiative and told me a joke to pass the time.

'What do you give a cannibal when he arrives late for dinner?' I knew it but shook my head like I had no idea. 'The cold shoulder,' he said, sort of serious.

He laughed then and I joined in, puzzled, but strangely touched by some subtle intimacy in his voice. I knew that he wasn't getting at me but I also knew that this joke was not spontaneous. What I wasn't sure about was why the joke seemed so appropriate. Then I realised that I must have told it to him years ago when he informed me earnestly one evening of his intention to become a vegetarian. I vaguely remembered telling him a whole bunch of stupid jokes and then asking him never to invite me round for dinner, or else I would have to come late with a burger and a bottle of whiskey.

I suddenly felt a flush of embarrassment, accompanied by a strange mixture of genuine affection and something close to pity for my sincere and healthy friend. He had obviously rehearsed this little scenario in his mind, or at least something close to it, to put me at ease when I arrived. I found it hard to believe that someone, anyone, could plan something so inconsequential and yet so effective, so intimate and so strategic at the same time, so caring and so calculated.

I felt immensely flattered and simultaneously patronised, and I had to fight back some unwelcome currents of emotion deep inside me. I struggled to keep calm, cool, myself, me, Myles, untouched, unfazed, cynical if necessary, mechanical, detached, in control. I didn't want this mixture of paranoia and sentiment, uncontrolled feelings and mental conflict – over what? A fucking vegetarian dinner, for Christ's sake. It was like I was sliding into the beginnings of a bad acid trip or a heavy dope buzz, where everything, every little thing, every word, movement and gesture becomes unbearably important and confusing. I knew that I was going somewhere I didn't want to go. Something was starting to slip. I had to resist, get back to Myles the Main Man. I poured some more whiskey and sipped at it, trying desperately not to look vulnerable, not to look stupid or weak. McNabb moved away. I lifted my dinner carefully and walked slowly into the living room, hot-fingered in one hand from the plate and cold in the other from the whiskey glass.

We settled down uncomfortably to watch some real-life news on the television, something I very rarely did due to my busy social schedule. I ate his healthy mush as enthusiastically as I could, feigning interest in the TV. I hated those tight-arsed talking heads who read the news, with their big world of clipped phrases and serious business. I could feel things getting tense as we sat in silence, allowing the television to cover for us, to postpone for us the inevitable discussion of our, my, nasty little world of thuggery and suspicion. McNabb waited politely until I set down the empty plate before he asked the obvious first question, about whether I had phoned Bigelow.

'I phoned him from the Green Room, and he told me, basically, to fuck off,' I replied, with maybe a bit too much emphasis on the Green Room, as if McNabb would automatically suspect that I had phoned from here, from his carefully protected headquarters. I had to be circumspect about what I said, what with this cloud of paranoia or guilt or whatever the fuck it was hovering around me.

'What exactly did he say?' He frowned after he said it. I knew he was going to ask that, and he knew that I knew.

'He said that business is business, but, in my case, he didn't care about the money. He said he wanted to make an example of me, for my friends, whoever they are. He said that he'd already given his fat boys permission to beat the shit out of me, and that was that.' I stopped.

'Is that it?' he said.

Fuck it, McNabb, my old sincere, intimate, calculating, relentless buddy – was that not enough? He looked at me hard, and I had to go on.

'He said that I sickened his shite, and his boys didn't like me either, for some reason.'

He almost laughed a bit, I thought, and then he collected himself. He loved to hear the old classic expressions, the old street slang, half-forgotten by him and long banished from his middle-class world. He frowned again, knowing that I could anticipate exactly what he was going to ask next.

'What did he mean? What reason?' He was getting impatient now.

'I dunno. They mustn't have liked the look of me, or didn't like my jokes, maybe.'

He dropped the interrogation, understandably enough, and went and got us some more whiskey.

When he came back he handed me the drink and then turned down the volume on the TV.

'I've been doing some checking up on these people,' he

said carefully. 'I got two of the senior men on my team to make some discreet enquiries with the cops and with a few guys on the ground, some loyalist ex-paramilitary types helping us a bit with our background information. These loyalist guys would know Bigelow and his employees pretty well. It won't surprise you to hear that Bigelow is shady, very shady, but clean. He wheels and deals in all kinds of stuff, mostly connected with property, and he definitely treats people like shit. But he stays within the law, as far as we can make out, and washes his hands of any nasty business. In other words, he's in a position to continue to do what he's doing without any legal interference. So, we, or anyone else, can't put pressure on him from that angle.'

It was pretty obvious from what he was saying that he, or his team, could influence the cops to put pressure on certain people if he wanted to – discreetly, of course. I wasn't too sure what to make of this, in terms of my image of McNabb and his unassailable personal integrity, but I was in no way surprised to hear about the RUC's flexibility in these matters. I said nothing and McNabb continued.

'The paramilitary types don't like him at all. They see him as a bloody nuisance, an exploiter of working-class people. But some of their friends or ex-friends, whatever the case may be, are still probably getting a lot of money from him, through protection payments and also for inside information about various deals within their communities. So, they won't want to get into anything messy with him unless it will pay dividends for them in the long run. And I'm afraid, Myles, I can't pretend that your case is anywhere on the list of possible trade-offs. Anyway, from what you've just said, if Bigelow doesn't care about the money any more, and wants to make an example of you, then it's become a different ball game.'

'Ball game? Yeah, with my balls in a sling as the end result,' I blurted out, and immediately felt like an idiot.

'You must have really annoyed him,' McNabb said, calmly but not very reassuringly.

'Yeah, I must have, right enough, and he deserved it. But now it's too late to pay the money back, even if I grovel. So, no matter what anyone tries to do, I'm still going to end up as a no-ball wonder at the end of it. Unless I do a runner. That's the only solution.'

'Where would you go?' he said simply. A simple question, indeed, with no ready answer.

'I dunno. I don't really know anybody anywhere else. I never thought about it properly. Maybe I should just take the beating and forget about it, only I think those two mountain men really want to hurt me for some reason. I don't get it. All I did was tell them a stupid joke. It must be because I'm a fenian, or something sectarian.'

'Tell me the joke,' he said, looking down at his whiskey, resigned.

I hesitated for a few moments to get my bearings. I realised, not for the first time, that I'd been snagged by my own story-telling technique, my neurotic tendency to edit differently for each occasion, to play to each particular audience, to distort or exaggerate, even when I was trying to tell the truth. I thought that I'd already told him the Bill and Ben joke as part of my original testimony the night before, but obviously not. I told myself for an instant that I must have left it out in my eagerness to provide a smooth, uninterrupted run in that part of the whole story. But I knew that there was something else going on. I knew that I'd fucked up again, that there was something important about the telling of this particular joke that I had sensed all along but wouldn't admit to myself.

'Tell me the joke,' he said again.

I swallowed some whiskey and told him the joke. He didn't laugh or smile or do anything remotely appropriate. He just sat there and stared at his glass, like a crystal ball cradled in his hands, revealing images that no one else wanted to see.

'They're gay,' he said quietly, and I let out a high-pitched little laugh, like someone deranged, like a fool, a simpleton, someone demented. What the fuck was happening to me? I immediately tried to regain some lost ground by forcing the laugh to continue a bit longer. I tried to deepen it, to twist it a bit, so to speak, into a knowing, indifferent sort of laugh, but it didn't work. It wasn't my style and McNabb was well aware of that. He gave me a long, sympathetic look, bordering, I could see clearly, on the patronising.

'They're not twins, they're brothers,' he continued. 'They've been living together for years in a small working-class neighbourhood in East Belfast, in a backstreet terraced house. They don't socialise or mix with anyone in the area, even though they were brought up there. They're weirdos, by all accounts, psychos probably . . .'

'Thanks,' I said. 'That's fucking great. That's all I need to know.'

'. . . and definitely gay, according to some people who were in contact with them years ago. Apparently they had a few seedy encounters way back in their early twenties, and everyone involved ended up in trouble, with family rows and disownments and all kinds of accusations flying around. But now they just hang out together and don't bother with anyone else. A cosy little set up, eh? All in the privacy of their own home, I suppose.'

I didn't respond.

'Everyone leaves them alone, and most people will say nothing about them, probably because they're afraid to. They have a reputation for real nastiness, if they're provoked. Bigelow took them on not long after he moved here from England. It's the perfect set up for both parties, it seems. They say nothing, ask no questions, do what they're told, and get paid good money for scaring the shit out of difficult tenants every now and again, and some-times worse. I don't know how much more you need to hear, Myles. These guys are violent.'

No response again. It didn't seem necessary. I knew everything already, in my guts. McNabb's delivery speeded up a bit, presumably to get the whole thing over with quickly.

'It seems that they enjoy both the money – they never had anything much before – and the work, according to some of their victims. The police were involved in some incidents but no charges were ever brought, for the obvious reasons. It's not hard to imagine the scenario. The cops are probably scared of them, as much as anyone, afraid to provoke them unnecessarily. Bigelow is probably nervous of them as well, which is why he tries to keep a distance from their activities. I'm surprised he didn't put them on to you sooner, to scare you a bit before things went too far – maybe it was because you wrote for a magazine . . .'

He went on for a while in a low voice, but I was frozen in time, stuck, fixated on the words 'provoke them unnecessarily'. What was this? Some kind of judgement call? It was like the so-called victims weren't worth the bother, not important enough, to warrant any action. By whose fucking standards? The cops', McNabb's, everybody's? That's the way it seemed. They were just no hopers, after all, weren't they? Bad tenants, people on the dole, loners, single mothers, students with no rich family connections, assholes of society, people who didn't fit in, bums and losers. I was in there among them for sure, a fucking useless bastard. A loser. A drunken shite. Loser, loser, drunken shite . . .

'All right,' I hissed. 'All right. I get the picture. Don't tell me any more, for fuck's sake.'

McNabb shut up and sat back in his chair. I went to the kitchen, brought out the bottle of whiskey and set it on the small table between us. No point in being too polite at this stage, I said to myself. He shook his head when I pointed the bottle at his glass, so I helped myself to a large measure. There wasn't much conversation for a long while after that, just a few comments from him about the nonsense on television, and a few comments from me about the nonsense everywhere.

'I can't pay them off,' I heard myself say eventually. 'It's too late. And I can't just disappear somewhere – my whole life is here, for what it's worth. Even if I did fuck off somewhere, they said they would get the Wife or my mates or someone else instead.'

McNabb glanced over and looked away again quickly. I guessed that I hadn't mentioned that specific point either in my previous account. I hadn't really done a very good job in putting him in the picture, the real picture that was. I was forced to conclude that my recounting technique fell short of the mark. It was weighed far too much towards the general and the theatrical, the overall drama of the event, rather than the detail. I was a shithead, in other words, wasting his time.

'I'm going to have to face up to them, fight them or take a beating. If I spend some time in hospital, it'll get me off the drink. I can still keep my job – I make most of that stuff up anyway, and I don't even bother going to most of the events I write about. It'll do me good in the long run. It'll keep me out of trouble. I can make a new start. Or maybe I can handle the bastards. I used to get into fights a lot when I was younger, when I played football, and I could handle myself pretty well. I was a tough kid . . .'

I talked away for a good while, complete nonsense, waffle for the hell of it. I was scared. I was really scared, and I didn't care any more if I sounded like a prat. McNabb would understand, he always did, and there was still a chance that he could do something, make things better. Some people could do that.

I must have polished off the whiskey and watched the television for a fairly long time after McNabb went off to bed at his usual hour.

Weeks later, when events had unfolded and I had more than enough time to think, I tried again and again to piece together the last fragments of that evening. I could remember boring him to death with my self-indulgent drivel. I could remember him getting up and leaving the room, and us both exchanging stilted goodnights. I could remember watching most of a really stupid TV movie about a jealous husband trying to catch his wife having an affair. I could remember brushing my teeth with striped toothpaste. I could remember staggering into bed. I could remember waking up with the cold sweats, sticky and wet, in the middle of the night. I could remember the thick grey fog in my head as I woke, the deeply resonating sense of unease. I could remember tossing and turning for the rest of the night, and most of the next morning. I could remember cursing everything and everyone I knew for putting me in this situation and for not helping me out. But I couldn't remember saying or doing anything specific to turn McNabb against me, to make him mad at me, mad enough to fuck me up worse than anyone else.

mex's place [5]

As soon as Mex left the flat to look for Matt I got on the phone to the Wife. I had to find out what she was doing in Nooks the night before, and whether the cops had been called after myself and Mex had fled the scene. I hoped the bouncer's jaw was broken, in three places with a bit of luck, slap it up the bastard, but I could do without any more complications. The last thing I wanted right now was the intrepid RUC joining the chase, tracking me down for violent crime.

The Wife's phone rang and rang and then the answering

machine kicked in. It was a new recording. I felt a little pang of jealousy when her voice declared, breezily and kind of seductively, that she was very sorry, she was not at home and that she would get right back to me, if I would leave a number. I thought for a second that it might be interesting to leave Mex's phone number, which was printed clearly on the casing of the phone in front of me. Mex and the newly seductive Wife might have a lot to talk about. They would have been a good match for each other anyway. But this was not the time for setting up a Myles Appreciation and Denigration Society. I needed to speak to her personally, so that's what I said to the machine. I added that I would phone again in two minutes, just in case she was there and was screening her calls. I tried again and hung up quickly when the flirty message started over.

I phoned McNabb's number, to be greeted again by an answering machine, this time brisk and business-like. I told the machine I would phone later. I was impatient and agitated when I started the calls and worse when I finished them. Now I was stranded in a prickly limbo, unable to move, unable to strike out in any direction, with too many questions still unanswered and everybody disappearing around me.

I tried to be positive. I got a beer from the fridge and put Miles Davis back on the CD player. 'We gotta run this voodoo down, Myles,' I said pointedly to the disc. I cleaned myself up a bit in the bathroom, and recovered the rest of my clothes. Then I sat and waited for what seemed like a long time, anxiously supping my beer, and trying to get a fix on the music, make a sanctuary of sound for my buzzing head. My mind wouldn't focus though, and the questions wouldn't give up so easily.

I couldn't help thinking very strange, mixed-up, but somehow perfectly logical, thoughts about what could be happening to Matt. He might have been sitting very comfortably in Nooks right at that moment, enjoying his beer and cigarettes and engaging in a good old one-sided chat about football with some unsuspecting customers. Or he could be wandering about somewhere just for the fresh air, or he might be with Mex in a coffee shop eagerly discussing the forthcoming photo session with his new lookalike buddy. But then again she was under strict instructions to phone me, was she not? Or . . . he could be in the hands of the fat red fucks, in which case my troubles could soon be over, depending on their powers of observation being none too sharp and his mouth being kept shut. Or something unexpected could happen, like him telling them where I was, and I would be in big shit very soon. I knew which option I was really, fearfully, deep inside of me, hoping for, but it was too much to contemplate the repercussions, and the attendant guilt.

The phone rang. I turned the music down, took a deep breath, and then slowly lifted the receiver. It had to be Matt or Mex. I knew then what kind of a bastard I really was when Mex's voice came on the line, and some instinctive force inside me gladly, almost cheerfully, marked up the increasing odds against poor old Matt.

She said that she was in McLaverty's and that she had decided to check a few bars around the area, bars that Matt was familiar with, just in case. He was nowhere to be seen. She hadn't been able to look into Nooks because our friend the bouncer was on duty again. He had a dark bruise around his chin, and a cut on his lip. He wouldn't let her in. He wouldn't speak to her apart from repeating like a fool that she was barred and couldn't come in. So she had no idea if Matt was in there or not. She reckoned he must be but, if that was the case, she didn't think he would stay too long. She said she was coming straight back to the flat to wait for him. I asked about the mountain men, and she gave a little snort, as if I was insane or something, and said she would be back in about ten minutes.

It was a long ten minutes. When she arrived back, she immediately helped herself to a beer and then perched, kind of distant, on the edge of the settee. She sat at one end, and I sat at the other, with a big solid space between us, and we sipped at our beers. I waited for her to say something. Eventually she asked me if I was all right, which took me by surprise. I said blankly that I was and asked her the same question. She looked at me hard and steady.

'What's wrong?' I said, to break the tension.

'What do you mean, what's wrong? How do you know those two assholes?' she said. 'What do they want from you? What are they snooping around Nooks for?'

My world was filling up with questions.

'One question at a time, if you don't mind.' I'd forgotten myself. I thought I was talking to the Wife for a second.

'Fuck off, Myles. What do they want you for?' She just brushed it off. I liked her for that.

'I owe their boss money. For rent I forgot to pay. A lot of money.'

'I thought so,' she said, followed by silence. I looked at her, quizzically, I suppose, what else could I do? And she looked back at me like a schoolteacher with all the facts at her fingertips. I didn't like that at all.

'What do you mean?' I said carefully, as I was meant to, just like in a script.

'Bigelow. He's my landlord, here and at the studio in town.'

My stomach churned violently, and I felt a steely taste in my mouth. I took some quick gulps of beer to steady the storm in my gut. I tried to look something other than stupid and panic-stricken, but I don't think it worked. Mex ignored the reaction and continued in an even voice.

'How do you think I got to know the two asshole brothers? They came round one day to the studio building to check up on one of the other artists who was renting a space there. He was way behind in his rent, and he moved out the day after their visit. He said that they were polite but firm, scary firm. Pay up or move out, they told him. They said Bigelow didn't want it to go any further, and it didn't. They didn't chase him for the money or anything. They took most of his pictures though. Bigelow is a slimy sort of character, but he's been a reasonable landlord to me and the other artists in the studios. I pay my rent and he takes care of repairs and things, and I never have any bother.'

I drank more beer. I couldn't believe what I was hearing. She kept on talking.

'I asked the two brothers to pose for photographs for my project. They're not twins but I fixed them up a bit, changed their hair and stuff to make them look as similar as possible and we did the photos, no problem. But after that they started to behave like twins, wearing the same clothes, and keeping their hair the same, and working on this weird routine of speaking in turns. I thought they were a bit simple, a bit nuts. Anyway, they came back to ask me for money for posing for the photos, and then asked me for some more later for the use of the images. I paid the money to get rid of them but they kept coming round to the studio to find out about the exhibition and about two artists I must have told them about, from London, who work as a gay couple. I started to think that they were gay, which made the whole thing weirder, but when I joked about it, kind of innocently – I mean it's nothing to me – they freaked out. They called me all kinds of names and stuff. Then they phoned here one night and insisted on calling round to ask me about the dates for my show. I got rid of them eventually but they scared me a bit, with their stupid routine and their creepy comments about my work. They said it was like a con game and that's why they liked it so much.'

I was sweating badly at this stage, and swallowing hard. They had been here in this apartment, maybe more than once. And Bigelow owned the fucking place. Mex continued to ramble on about her work and the fact that some of her twins weren't twins, and that it didn't matter, and what did they know anyway, it was art, and so on, but I wasn't listening any more. There were too many unwelcome movements in my gut. I was still trying to digest what she'd said about the fat bastards and about Bigelow. A reasonable landlord? Using me for a punch-bag, as an example, is fucking reasonable? Telling the two fat thugs to take their time and give me a good working over is reasonable? I had to interrupt her eventually to stop myself from choking on my own bile.

'Bigelow's a scumbag,' I shouted. 'The lowest of the low. An exploiter of the working classes. A fucking English landlord in Ireland. An asshole with no con-science, with no right to be here. A money-grabbing greedy capitalist bastard with two Irish monkeys, dumb enough to do his colonial dirty work . . .' I stopped to listen to myself. Was I really repeating this crap like I meant it? This was the kind of bullshit I would make fun of in my column, or more accurately, this was the sort of language I would use in my column as a pastiche to make fun of over-zealous and moralistic public figures. Christ Almighty, I was becoming my own fabrication, a cliché spouting clichés.

Mex was looking at me with her head at a slight angle, and then, when I didn't continue my diatribe, she must have registered the sudden and unexpected change in my expression. It must have been some spectacle. Self-righteous indignation to bafflement in one smooth milli-second, an almost impossible feat. She burst out laughing. And it was the same laugh – that open, unaffected, unre-strained laugh – I'd fallen in love with as she swayed and rolled against the wet hedge in the golden streetlight the night before. She soon stopped laughing, but kept on watching me intently. I was still grappling with clichés, different ones now, and she knew it. She moved over beside me and smiled and kissed me and I didn't resist. I just sat there wondering what to say next.

'I'm in big trouble,' I said after a while. 'I think I should go. Those fat fuckers could be on to me and I don't want anything to happen here.'

So much for having everything out with her, taking her to task, getting to the nitty-gritty, finding out what she was really all about. A resolute performance if ever there was one.

'Forget it,' she said quietly.'You're getting paranoid. We only met last night and nobody saw us come round here. No one knows you're here, except Matt, and he'll be back soon.'

Yeah, really, and where the fuck was he then? And who was he talking to? I really wanted to succumb to Mex's honey-crusted certainty, to play the happy fool, the innocent abroad, but I knew I wasn't getting paranoid. I was already paranoid. I couldn't help thinking about Bigelow the landlord and what kind of keys he might keep for his properties and who would have access to them. I shifted about uncomfortably. But I didn't want to go and she knew it. I didn't want to do anything. She grinned at me and she clinked her beer bottle against mine, like we were two old-timers, old drinking buddies with decades of bottle-clinking between us. Then she moved even closer to me and we sat and listened silently to the rest of the music. We would have to wait patiently for Matt and see what happened, there was no other option. That seemed to be the consensus she had arrived at without me, as I put my head back and stared at the ceiling.

'If Matt doesn't come back soon, we might have to forget about the photo session,' she said abruptly when the CD finished. She must have been mulling over the circumstances a bit more closely. I had drifted into a spell of relative acceptance, a semi-conscious state of listening, a vacant awareness of the slow shifts in Miles's tempo on the long last track, during which I could feel a deep drowsiness come over me. The sudden snap back to reality startled me awake, and I tried desperately to think of some way to keep things on an even keel.

'Is it important?' I asked, quickly. It sounded sincere. Clutching at straws was a long-time occupation of mine. 'The photo session, I mean.'

'Yes, it is,' she said, and started to tell me why. Then she stood up and stretched. She began at the beginning again and recited a litany of ins and outs, of whys and wherefores, of pros and cons about her twins project and its general implications for her work. I didn't want to hear about her work again, another fucking W word getting on my nerves. I wanted to interrupt, to tell her to give it a rest, but I also wanted to keep things as sweet as possible between us. So I kept quiet and pretended to listen.

As she went on I was surprised, and then amazed, to find myself paying more and more attention to what she was saying. On one level, it was a ridiculous charade, not in what she said, but in the contrived roller-coaster method of delivery, punctuated by sincere smiles and affectionate looks to encourage me along on her big intellectual trip. It was as if she had been rehearsing for months for this opportunity, and was making a heart-felt effort to get it exactly right. On another level, as the roller-coaster gained momentum I was gradually drawn in, I was enticed, I was held captive, I was entranced.

She talked and talked. I began to feel that something had happened in a place way beyond me, something important that I had completely missed out on. A realisation gradually forced itself on me that there was a deep gap in my perception of recent events, that some unusual rotation of the world had completely escaped me, that reality had transformed itself behind my back. I felt that I had deprived myself of something vital. I had robbed myself, sold myself short, as I blundered along in my drunken haze. I had conned myself and everybody else for years, smugly composing all that faked and fabricated nonsense for my so-called column. I'd wasted so much time looking for opportunities to attack whatever drifted into my blurry field of vision that I'd let all the real stuff pass me by.

As she talked, my penguin social life and my shared codes of conduct, where everything was reduced to a cynical laugh and a relentless pursuit of the ever-elusive good times, seemed more and more shallow and pointless. My whole existence took on a superficial gloss that became increasingly transparent, and then slowly cracked under the weight of her words.

At the beginning, it seemed like she was talking mostly nonsense, abstract bullshit, arty crap. Then it started to take shape, to form itself into crisp little pockets of sense, tiny chunks of logic, that gathered together and expanded into a cohesive structure. It grew and spread itself and developed its own momentum. It gradually evolved into a mass of pattern and connection that slowly, inexorably, solidified and crushed my fragile little world. And I could offer no defence, no possibility of reprieve, no way of going back.

I couldn't tell if she actually knew what she was talking

about, if she really had thought hard about all this stuff and hammered it out in her mind, bit by bit, line by line, but it didn't matter at this stage. It wasn't the meaning, it was the words. I'd heard them all before, from a reliable source, not so very long ago. I'd seen them in a glass, darkly. It was a *déjà vu* that broke my world, and left me with nothing – nothing but an eerie clarity, like the aftermath of a storm, and a flickering mental imagery that scared me half to death.

mcnabb's place [4]

When I forced myself out of bed and had a look at the daylight world of normality, I wasn't at all surprised. It was raining, a thin grey blanket of drizzle, monotonous and bland, and my good friend McNabb had gone off to work. He'd gone to negotiate with the bad guys and help make a better society for everyone in our unfortunate little country north of the big bad border. Fuck them all, I said to myself, especially the lying bastards of politicians, and the corrupt cops, and the sneaky buggers running around in the background. I lifted his note from the kitchen table. 'I'll see what I can do,' was all it said, in clear upright letters. Normally that would have given me some hope, some respite from the mental torture, but not today. Fuck what he could do or couldn't do. What difference would it make now? I'd had enough. I'd had more than enough. Today was the big day, decision day, D-day. D for done with it. I couldn't carry on like this any longer. I had to take a beating and get it over with. That was that. So be it. But it left a very limited range of options.

If I fought them, they would beat me more, and it was very possible, in their rage or frustration, they could kill me. They wouldn't be carrying guns, that would be far too dangerous for them, but they might be carrying weapons of some sort. Baseball bats were currently in fashion, but lead pipes, I'd been told, were the chosen means of punishment by non-paramilitaries. The cops recognised the signs and were less interested in such cases, such trivial little squabbles over debts or women or family honour, and the pipes were easily jettisoned and easily replaced. McNabb probably had a file somewhere on the hidden codes of cop-and-criminal interaction, and another one on the statistical probability for the use of various items in physical assaults on person or persons unknown.

If I took a dive, they would beat me like a cowardly cur, but they would be well satisfied with that outcome, as it would inevitably make them feel better about their prowess as fear-mongers and professional threateners. They would also get bored a lot quicker punching a dead weight, as opposed to a wriggling, screaming, flailing opponent. The punches might be more accurate but almost definitely fewer in number.

The second option was much more preferable to the first, so I settled conclusively on number two, as I tried to eat some of McNabb's home-made muesli with nuts and raisins.

The main problem of the day having been satisfactorily solved, I asked myself what else I could possibly think about to fill in the hours until the appointed time and place. Ah, time and place, the next problem. How could it have slipped my mind? Well, this was also a question of limited options. The easiest solution, in theory, was to phone Bigelow and make an appointment for a suitable time at a suitable venue for his boys to come and get me, and then casually beat me up. The snag was that he wouldn't believe me, and I would sicken his shite even more, and make things worse. The most practical solution was to go to the likeliest bar that I would usually frequent, or at least visit, on a Friday night and sit there until the mountain men came across me on their rounds, which they had to execute in order to find me. That was their job. All very logical. When they eventually found me, all I had to do was not run away and take my punishment like a man.

The bar that most satisfied the requirements was the Flatfield. So, that was the venue. And the time? It was now about midday, but I was in no hurry. If I spent the afternoon getting cleaned up and tidying up my things, that would be useful. It would be good to leave my room, and the bathroom and kitchen, in some kind of order. Then I could cruise down to the Flatfield about eight o'clock and take my time about everything. My fastidious friend McNabb would appreciate a neat and tidy home, and I might even have time to nip out for an hour or so to buy a few bottles of whiskey to replace the ones I'd polished off. He would appreciate that as well. Anything else? I didn't think so. That was just about everything taken care of. I could rest easy now that I had my day more or less planned out.

There was only one other problem, or maybe a few other problems. I had to run to the bathroom a couple of times, to throw up. And, every twenty minutes or so I got a fit of the shakes, worse than I'd ever had before. Ah, well. *C'est la vie.* This is this, and that's that, and that's the way the cookie crumbles.

mex's place [6]

M ex was talking up a storm, all right. The wise and ancient ones say that before a person can experience a spiritual renewal, he or she has to experience a breakdown of previous models, previous mindsets and patterns of behaviour. I was pretty sure that towards the end of Mex's extended exegesis on the ideas behind her work I was having a breakdown of sorts. But the strangest thing about it was, the more it developed, the more detached I felt from the whole process. It was like I was watching a slow-motion movie, with a strange soliloquy in progress, and as I sat entranced, a practically indiscernible flicker of subliminal imagery was playing mirror tricks with my mind. I was trying to focus on the way the central character had finally dragged the disparate units of her somewhat unwieldy account of years of intellectual effort into a relatively straight line, a parallel line, when she started to sum up.

'And that's why the duplication thing became more and more important for me. I used the twins as a sort of doubling of identity, as a model for duplication in nature. Then, when I ran out of twins I started looking for doppelgängers, and mixed them in with the twins. That gave another twist to the project. At first it seemed a bit dishonest but when I started making people look more like twins, like reproductions of themselves, by using make-up and stuff, it broadened the dimensions of the work. It made the whole thing more interesting. It was like I was making clones, but which was the original? Which was singular and individual and which wasn't? What was real, and what wasn't? It made perfect sense to mix them up and confuse things, because there is no pure perception of anything. It's all relative to something else. So reality can never be captured. That's the basic idea behind all my work – the earlier work as well, the installations with the projections and the mirrors. Do you understand what I'm getting at, Myles, or am I going on too much?'

She smiled at me and I smiled back.

I paused and dug into my memory. I pictured McNabb in his living room with a whiskey glass in his hand, talking steadily. I wanted to get this just right.

'I understand,' I said slowly. 'The investigation of reality through any system automatically involves a distortion of that reality. Every duplication or fabrication is naturally a distortion, a deception. Therefore the understanding of any so-called reality must entail a pattern of deception, and so reality, as we know it, is a deception. Reality can never be captured.'

She laughed and hopped about, ecstatic and astounded, for a few seconds. Then she gradually came back to reality, our reality, the reality of our brief history, of me and her, especially me. She stopped jumping around and stared at me.

'Are you taking the piss?' she said.

Of course I was. What else could I do? She'd left me no other alternative. McNabb's garbled logic was my last option.

'Did that sound like taking the piss? Did that sound like a joke to you? Well, did it?' I asked.

'No,' she said.

I repeated my summary, with a little paraphrasing, to emphasise the complete and unshakable grasp I had on the ideas we were discussing. She smiled a big happy smile.

'So, where do me and Matt fit in?' I asked politely. I could barely mention his name without a barrage of horrific images flashing into my head and spoiling the slow-motion movie. I forced myself to concentrate.

'You and Matt are the last doppelgängers. I need one more image. When I get your photograph done, that will even off the numbers, create a symmetry in the number of large pictures I'm planning to show. I didn't think I would be able to do it in time, so to answer your first question, yes, it is important to me. There are other artists out there dealing with the same issues, at least similar issues, and so I have to make this exhibition count. It's a big thing for me. A friend of mine is writing the catalogue essay for the exhibition. He's a well-known painter, and he has dealt with mirroring and reflex images in his own work. I can't wait to talk to him now that I'm getting this stuff clearer in my mind . . .'

It was clear in my mind, at this stage, that my life would never be the same again. My head felt so clear that the light in the room was pressing on my brain. It was crystal clear, for starters, that I was being used. Sympathy fuck or no sympathy fuck, I was a simple flat-footed, empty-headed patsy, an expendable item, a wooden block to complete the symmetry of Mex's little edifice. I was a mere duplication, a fabrication, a deceit. But that was just the beginning. It became clear that I was a fabrication, an object of complicit deceit, for everyone else as well. I had fooled them and they had fooled me. I wasn't real for the Wife, or for the Lads, or even for McNabb. I was someone they made up, a reflection they needed to complete an image of themselves, someone that could be remodelled or dropped when a better image came along. It was all a waste of time, a stupid and pointless game of interdependency, as McNabb had said. I didn't really matter to any of them. The real me, another deceit, no doubt, wasn't even a flea, an irritation, that could get noticed in the game. The real Myles was a flea's flea, a tiny reflection within a tiny reflection, invisible, too far distant to make out.

For some reason, the movie script didn't allow me to get

upset or angry, like I should have been, just detached and disappointed, and a bit dizzy. The subliminal imagery was speeding up, moving into the empty spaces where my sense of myself used to be. More and more images, featuring my doppelgänger, were coming at me thick and fast, and they were throwing me off balance.

'. . . you've helped me a lot , Myles, just by listening.'

I smiled weakly, and rose to get another beer. I knew there was one last bottle left in the fridge and I needed it. I went to put on some music, but I stopped short in front of the hi-fi, caught in a trance. My mind was somewhere else. I stared into the mirror. I moved away.

Mex said something about cooking some food, but I wasn't hungry. She banged around in the kitchen, pulling things out of cupboards and drawers, and I wanted desperately to leave. I wanted to feel something tangible, something real. I wanted the sharp taste of whiskey. I wasn't sure how long I could stick the incessant cutting and chopping and thumping. My mind was throwing up images I didn't want to see, as she rinsed and pulled and diced and dipped. And twisted and sliced and dragged and scraped. And crushed and squeezed and gouged and split.

I was pacing up and down, just out of her line of sight, when the phone rang. She was stirring something noisily on the cooker, so she shouted at me to answer the call. She added that it was probably Matt and that I should tell him to come straight back. I knew it wasn't Matt. But I didn't have much choice in the matter. I lifted the receiver carefully and said nothing.

'Your new boyfriend's in the alley behind Nooks,' the

squeaky voice said. 'He's not so good-looking any more.'

The line went dead, just like in the movies, in an endless reflection of movies within movies, and I hung up after a while. I went back to drinking my beer. I was all fucked up.

'Was it Matt?' she asked, very loudly. 'Where is he?'

'We have to go out,' I said suddenly, as I lifted my coat. 'Come on.'

I ignored the questions and the protestations and the fuss about the food and the cooker. I went down to the street and stood at the kerb, not even bothering to look around. It was raining, soft and light. Mex came down eventually, still protesting and shouting questions at me. I walked off in the direction of Nooks and she followed, all flapping arms and flapping mouth. I turned abruptly into the alleyway behind the hotel as she tried to pull at my arm.

We found Matt quickly enough, sitting crumpled on the ground against a rusty drainpipe bolted to the wall. He was sandwiched between two large refuse containers on wheels, with plastic bins scattered all around, so that no one could see him from either end of the entry. There was a stream of bloody water running away from him, streaked with shades of red and rust and oily residues. His hands were bound roughly behind his back with some kind of heavy tape and he was secured to the drainpipe by a leather belt, probably his own, pulled tightly round his neck, half-choking him. He was groaning and coughing and gasping for air, trying to call for help, and he was dripping and spitting blood everywhere. There was something black on his head, partially covering his face, but I could see that his nose was all smashed up, and his mouth was in a mess. It also looked like one of his legs was badly broken below the knee. Mex started screaming and rushed at him. She shoved one of the containers back out of the way, kicking and swearing at it. She started pulling and jerking and fumbling around, trying frantically to undo the belt, screaming and cursing the whole time.

I leaned in behind her. I pulled the black shape off his head as gently as I could, and stepped back to stare at it. It was a mask, similar to the Lone Ranger's but without the eye-holes, something that could be used as a sexual gimmick, although it wasn't intended as such. It was intended to help someone sleep in the light of a streetlamp filtering through cheap bamboo blinds. It was covered in watery blood.

I stood and watched as Mex undid the belt and then struggled to free Matt's hands. She screamed at me to help, but I just stood there holding the mask, trying to think. Matt choked and spat and tried to form words. Mex unravelled part of the tape and got his hands free. She cursed and cried and implored him to take it easy but he kept on gasping until he got the words out.

'You fucker, you set me up,' he managed to croak through blood and spit.

He was looking at Mex. I was right behind her and it was hard to tell through all the mess on his face, but I knew he was looking at Mex.

She jumped up and rounded on me. She screamed into my face.

'What did you do to him, you fucking bastard? What did you do? How did you set him up, you fucker? Look at him. Look at him, you fucking animal, you creep. Look what you've done. Look at him.'

I turned away. I started to run. I held on to the mask and ran, slipping and splashing in the rain. Some trendy girls, out early for their Saturday night fun, were standing at the end of the alleyway, listening to the screams and curses. They scattered when they saw me run at them. As I rushed past I shouted for them to get an ambulance quick, someone was hurt, and I pointed to the bins. I ran and staggered and pushed past people until I reached the taxi depot near McLaverty's. I jumped into the first taxi and barked at the driver that it was an emergency. I gasped out the address. I think he already knew, when he saw me swerving frantically towards the depot, to keep his mouth shut and say nothing. We took off fast.

I had to get to the Wife's place in a hurry. If she wasn't at home, I was in the deepest shit I would ever be in.

the flatfield

I pushed open the main door of the Flatfield bar and looked inside. I took my time and did a good survey of the bar and its occupants before I stepped in. No point in rushing anything. There were a few scattered groups and some solitary drinkers – it was still too early for most people, normal people. I said hello to some of the punters, nodding and smiling like I meant it, and ordered a pint at the bar. I could see three of the Lads, a trio of notoriously fast drinkers, sitting in the far corner. They looked like they'd been in the bar all afternoon. They were raw and ragged, and they were having a great time howling at each other. I waved over but they hardly noticed.

I was in no hurry to join them, so I stood at the bar and drank my pint quickly to help with the shakes. I'd been very tempted to down a few whiskeys from McNabb's newly restocked supply, before I'd left his house. He would be surprised to come home from work and find three unopened bottles in his spotless kitchen. But I had forced myself to do without. I was desperately trying to be sensible. I kept telling myself that I was going to take a serious beating tonight. I was going to take a beating and I didn't want to be so drunk that I would throw up if I was rendered unconscious, which was very possible, and choke to death on my own vomit. And I didn't want to piss myself either. How sensible can you get?

I gripped the bar to stop my hands shaking. Then I felt like an idiot. No one would even notice. And if they did, they would assume it was just another hangover symptom, not worth commenting on, except maybe to slag me about showing off my hard-bitten life style. I told myself to relax, I had a while to go yet, a few hours, maybe, before I was beaten to a pulp. I got another pint and joined the Lads. They all grunted and said hello, penguin-style, and I felt superficially at home. Soupey and Bap, inseparable lifelong mates, were already extremely drunk. I wondered how long they would last before they collapsed completely. Jonty, the third of the group, looked like he could handle a conversation, so I pushed my way in beside him.

'All right Myles? How's it hanging?'

'Sticking out,' I said, and we started up a banter about

nothing in particular, about other bars and parties and drinking sprees. Soupey and Bap shouted and joked at each other and then at us, and eventually, every time I opened my mouth to say something, they hollered at me to get real and catch myself on. Then they would burst into maniacal laughter. It was only some stupid running joke they had going, but I began to imagine that even harmless drunks sensed something vulnerable about my body language and felt obliged to pick on me. Under different circumstances I would have been very happy to sit there and suffer the friendly abuse, but I kept watching the door and I couldn't settle. My brain was all over the place, and my guts were as tight as hell. I started drinking more than I should have done, but it was impossible not to, with the Lads ordering pints left, right and centre.

The bar began to fill up, and the noise level and ambient smoke increased dramatically. At some stage in the evening Marty, another buddy with sound drinking credentials, appeared through the door, wet with rain, and made his way gradually to our table, which was now covered with a surfeit of pints and a lake of spillage. He took one look at Soupey and Bap and helped himself to one of their pints from the table. It dripped all over his jacket as he took a quick swallow.

'What's the difference between Soupey and Bap and a terrorist?' he asked.

Everybody knew that one but I let him finish.

'You can negotiate with a terrorist,' he said with a grin, and took another swig from the pint. He looked at me, and proclaimed meaningfully, 'I'm going to emigrate.'

'Why?' I had to ask. He sat down.

'Because of this fucking rain, and the fucking peace process, and the fucking stupid political negotiations. They're all going to go on for ever. And I think you should come along with me, my old mucker, before you get into any more bother. You're living dangerously, messing with the wrong people.'

'What are you talking about, Marty?' I had to ask, again. It was part of the routine, but I really didn't like the way he was looking at me, as if he knew something I didn't. Most of the mates would have heard by now about Bill and Ben chasing me, but I'd kept the real facts to myself. Whatever you say, say nothing, that's what they say.

'I hear you're in a bit of trouble,' he answered. 'You need some help with your negotiations. I know the two boys who are looking for you, and I could put in a word, if you like. I know them pretty well. They're decent characters really, they're just annoyed at you for causing them to lose some handy bits of work they needed at the time.'

'What the fuck are you on about? How do you know those bastards?' I was amazed at his stupidity.

'They're not bastards, I just told you that. They're mad at you, that's all. I can have a word with them and it'll be sorted out, no problem. You can buy us all a few pints and it'll be grand, you'll see, as right as fucking rain. They should be in here later this evening. They're working on a new job just around the corner and they were in here the other night. Your name came up in the conversation and they said they were going to knock your bollox in, if they came across you. But they're not usually like that. They're hard as nails but there's no real harm in them. I told them I knew you and that you were a decent spud, and then they sort of changed the subject. They're just mad at you, but they'll come round if I talk to them.'

'Fuck you,' I said and I meant it. This was no joking matter. 'You're talking complete shite, Marty. They're fucking assholes.'

'Fuck you too, Myles. I know these guys. Do you want me to get them off your back, or not? All it'll take is a serious good word from me and a few pints from you. Well? Yes or no?'

Soupey and Bap started to shout at the two of us to get real and catch ourselves on. Jonty wanted to know who owned what pints, and whose round it was, and what the fuck was going on with the drink. The noise in the bar suddenly got louder. My head started to buzz, and my nervous system crackled with fire. I could feel my stomach going somewhere. I made a bolt for the toilets and threw up half a gallon of black stuff in an open cubicle. Somebody at the urinal shouted 'Geronimo' and started to laugh. I didn't look up for a while. This was becoming a bad habit. I rinsed out my mouth and washed my face. At least I wouldn't be getting too drunk, I thought, but I felt embarrassed and ashamed – this was one of the worst crimes imaginable in the Flatfield.

I went back to the company, sat down, scooped a pint off the table and pretended nothing had happened. Marty was watching me closely, still waiting for an answer. I nodded yes to him and said nothing. What could I say? I didn't know what was going on. He was full of shit but he was usually straight with his mates. Maybe, just maybe, he knew something I didn't know, and maybe he really could do something to bale me out.

I didn't have to wait too long to find out. Within five minutes, there was a noticeable hush of voices near the main door, the kind of temporary suspension of chatter that happens when strangers come in to a neighbourhood bar like the Flatfield and everyone stops to stare at them. I looked over and felt the hair stand up on the back of my neck. It was the ugly red bastards all right, dressed in black, like the last time, but bigger and meaner looking than I remembered them. I gulped at my drink. They moved slowly to the edge of the bar and glanced around cautiously through the fug of smoke. I sat still and tried not to move, not to duck or hide. One of them noticed me and touched the other one on the arm. I thought I could see a little smile on his fat face. I stayed still. I wanted it to be finished, all over with. Or I wanted Marty to do something. I wanted him to prove he wasn't just a bullshitter. I wanted him to perform a miracle, to manufacture a glorious last minute twist in the plot so the hero gets saved and we all have a few pints and go home happy and victorious. I kicked him under the table to get his attention.

'There they are,' I hissed, and pointed my pint in their general direction. 'Just like you said they would be. So, go and talk to them, and save my arse.'

He looked over towards Bill and Ben, and screwed up his face.

'Where?' he said.

'Over there, you blind cunt,' I shouted, much to the amusement of Soupey and Bap and some of the other drinkers in the close vicinity. 'The two fat gits with the ginger hair.'

'Them?' he said. 'That's not them. They're just two twin wankers who started to come in here in the last couple of days. They have one drink and leave. They must have moved into a flat or something nearby, maybe one of the flats across the road just renovated by that fucking property developer, what's his name, Bigelow. He's the plonker my two mates used to work for.'

Christ Almighty, when would it end?

the wife's place

The taxi driver mustn't have noticed the blood-stained mask in my hand, or he would have told me politely to fuck off before I got in the car. Either that or he was new on the job and was too timid to offend a customer. The second option soon appeared to be the more likely case. He did what he was told and got a move on, but he didn't know the quickest way and kept asking me for directions. In my mental confusion, I barked out one or two wrong instructions and we ended up screeching round bends and through junctions, trying to work out the fastest route. I sat in the back and whimpered and snapped, and generally put the fear of God into him.

I turned the mask gingerly around and around in my hands as we raced through the city. I was mumbling and talking to myself, and putting on a good show of being demented, which wasn't surprising really, given what I'd just seen in that alley. Poor bastard, that could have been me, I kept saying, that should have been me. Matt's angry, frightened, blood-soaked eyes kept flashing across my vision every time I looked down at the mask. I found some old tissues in my coat pocket and tried to clean the blood off the wet fabric. The tissues started to break up and stick to my fingers, and then stick to the surface of the mask. It became a bloody, gooey mess, just like Matt's face. I asked myself why I was doing this. I didn't know why I hadn't dumped it immediately – I always hated the fucking thing anyway.

I tried to analyse why I'd held on to it, why I was still holding on to it, why it was so important to me. It obviously reminded me of the old days, but it started to take on a more subtle cast. I saw it as symbolising the Wife's selfishness, or self-sufficiency, or independence, I couldn't tell exactly what, but it involved a blindness to my needs, that was certain. Then I began to see it more as a symbol of our blindness towards each other. So, there I was, cleaning blood that should have been mine, that was spilled through blindness, off a black mask, a symbolic relic of a marriage destroyed by blindness, in a taxi speeding blindly to save my ex-loved one from some predicament I was blind to, and I was trying to analyse the situation. If I was still in a movie, and it felt like it somehow, it was a deeply pretentious and ridiculous art-house flop. My brain was in a meltdown condition, collapsing in on itself. I was now trying desperately to analyse the analysis of the analysis. I told myself to wise up, to catch myself on. I started thinking again about my need for psychiatric treatment and that did the trick – I knew that when someone really goes over the edge, they never think about getting medical help. I threw the torn and fragmented tissues out the taxi window. I hesitated for a few seconds and then I threw the mask out after them. It caught in the wind and flew up and soared into the air and disappeared. I started to focus again.

I tried to clean my hands as best I could. I gave the driver some precise and accurate directions, in a steady voice, and I think that calmed him down. His driving improved enormously. As we approached the house I searched around for a tenner to give him, a generous tip by way of compensation for the gunky particles of red and white stuff stuck to his back seat. I didn't know what I was going to do if the Wife wasn't there. The taxi came to a halt at the front of the house, just behind a large, dark blue car. I recognised it immediately. What the fuck was McNabb doing here?

I rang the bell and waited, and wiped my hands roughly on the rain-soaked ivy growing up around the doorway. I noticed how fresh and luxuriant it looked, compared to the under-nourished, spindly, creepy thing I remembered from not so long ago. McNabb answered the door and looked away when he saw me.

'Hi Myles,' he said softly. 'We've been trying to find you.'

'I've been busy,' I answered. 'Is she here? And what are you doing here?'

'I told you, I've been looking for you . . .'

I think he was going to say some more, but we were interrupted by a loud screeching and thumping down the stairs, obviously precipitated by the sound of my voice.

'You bastard. You fucking selfish, stupid bastard,' the Wife screamed, as she threw herself at me, arms swinging, aiming for my head. She was in one piece anyway, that was for sure, and as fit as a fiddle, as far as I could make out. McNabb pulled her back, and told her to cut it out, that it wouldn't do anybody any good. He didn't sound very convincing. He led her into the living room, holding her by the elbow as she twisted and turned, in little jerks, to get at me. He tried to get her to sit down, but she stood glaring at me, and cursed me under her breath.

'It's just as well you're here,' McNabb said, and he looked cautiously in my direction.

It wasn't like him to look at people like that, sideways, shifty, guilty of something. I knew immediately, instinctively, what had happened. I couldn't believe it, but I knew it must have happened. I stared at him and he looked away. He mumbled something to the Wife, but before he could say any more, I pointed my finger at her.

'You bitch,' I spat. 'You slept with him, didn't you?'

'Fuck you,' she spat back. 'What do you care? Who was that tart you were with last night in Nooks? Some young whore, a right little scrubber, by the look of her. And the state of you, you fucking idiot, you looked like a lunatic, like someone demented, with your hand stuck up a tart's dress in the middle of a public bar. You're a fucking disgrace . . .'

Her voice got louder, and she started shouting and screaming about me and my stupid, selfish, drunken ways. Then she suddenly launched into a whole rigmarole about the two fat fucks calling there the night before and getting her out of bed, and about being pushed around and humiliated, and about her money disappearing, and about being scared out of her wits, and about them stealing her mask, and about getting dressed and rushing down to Nooks to save my stupid ass.

Old habits die hard, I thought briefly, as she launched into a renewed barrage of abuse about my drinking. I heard about half of it. It seemed for a while that we were back in time, standing in our living room repeating the same scenario we had repeated before, hundreds of times, and that nothing had changed. Except that McNabb was standing ghost-like in the blue corner, a witness to the slaughter, a shadowy and reluctant referee, not doing a very good job. Eventually he intervened and told her to hold on and let me talk. She slowed down a bit. He asked her a few more times to let me speak, and then he asked me quietly to explain what happened last night.

'Explain?' I said.

She shut up at last.

I leaned against the wall and looked at them both standing there like tensed-up assholes, guilty parties, partners in crime against me. I felt bad, very bad, worse even than in the taxi. I didn't know what to say, or how to say it, or why I should even bother trying to say anything. It was too late. It was far too late for explanations, so what was the point? Everything went quiet for a few seconds. Nobody moved. I wished the Wife would start up again to stop me from thinking about her and McNabb. She just stared at me silently and I used the opportunity to push myself towards the door, out through the hall and on to the front step, into the rain. I started to walk away for good, for ever. That was it. I was finished.

I could hear some more shouting and McNabb's voice telling her, reassuring her, that he would be back, maybe in an hour or so, or he would phone her, and then he came running after me.

'Myles, hold on, we have to get this sorted out,' he kept saying, pleading with me to stay where I was while he got the car, and then we could drive around or go somewhere to have a talk, and get things cleared up. I didn't want to talk about anything, but he kept on and on, until I stopped walking away.

'Right. Get the car and we'll go for a drink,' I said. He nodded and told me to wait there.

He ran to the car and jumped in. He swung it around quickly, pulling up beside me. I took off my coat, and threw it into the back as I climbed into the passenger seat.

'Where do you want to go?' he asked.

'The Lock bar,' I said simply. I could feel his eyes staring at the side of my head.

'I don't want to go there,' he said calmly.

'Too bad,' I answered. 'That's where we're going if you want to talk.'

He didn't say anything for the rest of the journey, but I could tell by the first two or three turns of the car that we were going to the Lock. He must have realised I was being completely perverse, and he must have hated me for it, but he said nothing. He just drove towards the bar that he feared most, that he avoided at all costs, the site of our first encounter, the place where his life almost ended.

the flatfield [2]

Bill and Ben ordered what looked like plain cokes and paid the barman, who made some remark to them. He must have had them pegged as two big country boys recently arrived in the city. If he'd known anything about their real backgrounds, they would never have got through the front door. They said something in response. It was all part of their job, I supposed, to pretend to barmen that they were regular human beings just getting along and trying to have a good time like everybody else. They probably gave each barman a few bob extra, or told him to have a drink on them, as part of their programme of extracting information the easy way, and, of course, every one of the bastards probably went along with it, as nice as ninepence and as friendly as a ten-pound note.

The fat shites stood plumply against the bar and had another good look around. I couldn't help wondering how they planned these situations, whether they had a range of patterns to work to, or whether it was just simply a question of find, grab, and beat. I wondered if they had contingency plans for expected deviations from the normal routine. If I jumped up and ran for the door, for example, would they try to stop me and risk the attention of the entire bar, or would they follow me out quickly and try to apprehend me on the street? Did they have their car parked right outside, ready for a possible chase? If I suddenly produced a weapon, say a broken bottle, and three mates to back me up, would they risk a bar-room brawl? If I burst into tears and begged for mercy, would they be embarrassed? I could have occupied myself all night with dumb questions and idle speculation, but my nerves were grinding themselves into tatters. So I got up from my seat and moved away from the table.

'Where are you fucking off to, like royalty?' Marty was calling after me.

'Nowhere,' I said. I walked unsteadily through the crowd towards Bill and Ben. I wasn't drunk. In fact, I was perfectly sober. But I was shit scared.

They looked at each other and then looked around the bar again, as if they were suddenly aware of a scenario they hadn't anticipated, maybe an ambush of some sort. They watched me carefully as I got closer to them, and one of them stepped sideways a bit and squared off to make room for whatever was going to happen. The other one smiled at me, a stupid knowing kind of smile.

'Take it slow, fuckhead, and say nothing,' said the squeaky voice, quietly enough to spare the nearby punters any unnecessary affront to their sensibilities. 'You're leaving with us.'

'OK, Bill,' I said. I couldn't help it, my nerves were bad. It just slipped out.

'Funny cunt to the end, eh? You won't be so fucking funny when we get you out of here,' Ben said and nodded to Bill to walk ahead.

I thought about outside and I could feel my bladder going. I fought hard to control it. That would have been worse than a beating, to disgrace myself like a scared rabbit in front of the whole bar. That would have been a great story for every pint-swigging wanker in Belfast for years to come, for generations to come – the night that the supposedly cool, streetwise hombre, Myles the Mouth-piece, pissed himself with fear in the Flatfield bar. I squeezed and contracted internal muscles I never knew I had, to hold back the flow. I was still holding tight when Ben nudged me in the back to start moving towards the door. The bladder crisis passed as quickly as it began, minus a mischievous drip or two, and I thanked some unknown force for saving me a little dignity in the midst of my troubles. The unknown force wasn't finished with me yet, though.

All three of us turned in unison, with Ben's fist in my back, and shuffled slowly through the crowd towards the door. As we approached, it was pulled outwards and through it stepped two familiar figures, still joking with some people behind them in the entrance. Their cheerful, laughing faces froze into cold stares when they saw us.

'Look who it is,' one of them said loudly. 'Myles the Moaner, and look who's with him. If it isn't the ginger pricks, Bigelow's big tough boys.'

'What are you doing round here, boys? Looking for somebody to beat up?' said the other one, obviously addressing the fat pigs, but looking at me. 'Seems like you've got someone. Remember us, Myles?'

I remembered them all right. It was the two builders who worked on the dump I rented from Bigelow. My memory raced back to the damp flat with the mysterious leaks that never seemed to get fixed no matter how much work was done to them, that infamous flat where all the complaints were made about the incompetence of the builders, the same builders who were eventually sacked by their miserable employer. I remembered them as merely bit players in my big drama at the time – I had meant no harm to them and I really didn't think that Bigelow would sack them so readily.

They were both looking at me like I was a piece of dogshit on their best boots. I tried to say something, to let them know it was nothing to do with them personally, to make a grand statement of my innocence, of my lack of malice towards them, but I only got as far as the first stuttered word. Before the second word came out of my mouth, Bill punched me in the stomach with the back of his hand and knocked the breath out of me. I buckled up a bit and clutched my gut, and I didn't see exactly what happened after that.

I distinctly heard one of the builders telling Bill to back off, that he wanted a word with me, and only me, on my own. Bill told him to mind his own fucking business. Ben was pushing me in the back so that I nudged against some nervous punters nearby and caused them to spill some drink. They started hollering at everybody to take it easy, and Ben jerked me sideways, probably thinking I was trying to escape. At the same time, Bill must have attempted to force himself past the builders to clear a path towards the door. One of them pushed him back hard and shouted something. Bill slammed into me and Ben rushed forward and threw a punch. Everything suddenly fused together in a blast of noise and frantic movement, heavy bodies bouncing off each other and fists flying in all directions. There was a hell of a lot of shouting and screaming in the background, and drinks crashing every-where. I was knocked around by swinging elbows and flailing arms, and ended up falling backwards on the floor, away from the main pack. I was trying to get up when Marty's face appeared above mine. He grunted loudly as he pulled me upright.

'You're a shit negotiator, Myles,' he said. 'You better fuck off pronto.'

For a split second I thought about staying and taking my medicine like a man, but I could hear howls of pain. So I changed my mind and fucked off as pronto as I could. They were still at it, heaving and hauling, pushing and punching, as I struggled to find a path towards the door. Punters were ducking and diving everywhere, trying to save their drinks, and glasses were rolling and crunching on the floor. Above the racket I could make out Soupey and Bap hollering for everybody to get real and catch themselves on, and then howling with laughter. Jonty was shouting at them to shut up. Marty struggled along with me, shielding me a bit from the crushing bodies, urging me to push harder in the general direction of the door. As we reached the exit, there was a noticeable subsidence in the noise level. I looked back and saw Bill and Ben rise up almost simultaneously, as it were, from the scrum. There were at least four people on the floor, writhing about, and some others stumbling over them and around them. One of the mountain men saw me and started to move towards us, tripping and staggering as he went, and the other followed his movements immediately. I rushed outside with Marty just behind me. He yelled at me to hurry up and pointed to a taxi parked just along the road. I raced towards it, skidding on the wet road. Marty shouted after me as I ran.

'I told you they'd come,' he roared. 'I'll talk to them later. You owe me a couple of pints.'

the lock

McNabb drove slowly into the carpark at the Lock. I could feel him tense up as he swung the car around, alongside the railings separating us from the Lagan. He swung around again into a convenient parking space near the entrance to the bar, facing away from the river. I got out and walked quickly through the main door. The bar was quiet. There were some empty seats scattered about. I found two and pulled them as far away from other people as I could get, to a small ledge in the corner, and waited for McNabb to join me. He got me a pint and, for himself, a pure orange juice, very wholesome, very natural, and sat down opposite me. He was nervous at first and kept shifting around in his seat. I supped at my pint and said nothing, so he had to do all the talking.

He started off by telling me that it wasn't his fault, that he had tried to keep things under control, in proper order, as he described it, but that they both drank a lot of whiskey and things got out of hand. Probably my fucking whiskey, I thought, bought with the Wife's stolen money. That was a typical scenario – bad karma packed together in three tight little bottles of retribution, spiritual nemesis. Then he stopped and said that maybe he should start at the beginning, especially if I was determined to make it hard for him, and sit there and say nothing. I said nothing.

He talked it all out, talked it all away, without me saying a word. He went through the whole thing, pretty much in detail, while I slouched back in my seat and slowly drank my pint. He broke off near the middle to get us two more drinks, the same again, and then continued where he'd left off. He started from when he had come back from work the evening before.

'It was a lot later than usual, after a hard day. I was relaxed and half-asleep in front of the television when the phone rang. I thought it might have been you, otherwise I wouldn't even have answered it. I was kind of worried after what you'd said the night before about taking a beating and so on, even though it seemed like you were just letting off steam.'

He stopped here. I didn't react, so he kept on talking, sliding into a slow, business-like, steady voice. He was getting into his part now, his explicator role.

'It was your wife on the phone, asking for you, and then she started raving like a madwoman about the two fat men coming to her house. I eventually got her to calm down a bit, and asked her how come she'd phoned me. She told me straight away that there was a call to her work one morning, from you, and that you had left a message. She checked the number you'd phoned from and noted it down. She said that it seemed kind of familiar but not a number she could place. She had gone through her pocketbook later and discovered it was my number, almost buried away from years ago, with my address.'

He looked at me for a while, again expecting something, some reaction. I stared into my pint and showed no response, no sign of remorse, so he continued.

'She said that it was an emergency. She was convinced that you were in real trouble this time, and she was scared out of her wits. Two men had just come to her house and got her out of bed. They pushed her into the hallway when she answered the door, and grabbed some mask out of her hand, something she used for sleeping, I don't know exactly what it was. Anyway, they made fun of it and took it away with them, for some weird reason.'

I fought back a turmoil of mental images.

'Then they pushed her about a bit and told her that they'd had enough of you, and so on. They'd just come away from a serious bit of bother in the Flatfield bar because of you, and it was the last straw. They told her that you owed a lot of money and that she had better help them to find you. She had offered them money, and went to get some from a biscuit tin, where she hid her spare notes. It was empty, apparently, and she reckoned that you'd taken it.'

I still said nothing.

'They laughed at her and tried to get her to tell them where you were staying. She told them she didn't know, but she could have told them very easily, Myles, very easily.'

He hesitated for emphasis, through force of habit, no doubt, from his training in smooth delivery. But he'd probably realised, at this stage, that it was a waste of time to expect any kind of reaction, and he didn't get one.

'Anyway, they left eventually. They told her that they might have to call again and not to be bothering the poor overworked RUC in the meantime or things would get worse. She phoned me almost immediately, but what could I do? I tried to calm her down, but I couldn't do anything. I didn't want to get directly involved. Sorry . . .'

Yeah, I thought, fuck you too.

'I advised her to stay at home and do nothing, just lock the doors and sit tight, that it was safe now, and I would drive over in the morning, this morning, to talk to her. She said she couldn't just stay there, she was too scared, for herself and for you, and she hung up. Apparently she went off to warn you. She went to McLaverty's and then Nooks, and there you were with some girl, carrying on like there was nothing wrong, like you were on holiday or something. So, there was a big scene. Just after you left, the fat guys arrived and she hid somewhere. She saw them talking to the bouncer for a few minutes, and then they disappeared . . .'

That was it, the missing piece. That poxy bouncer knew

Mex and told them that I was with her. But then they would have gone round immediately to her flat. Jesus Christ, they did – they must have been in that fucking car that stopped for a while on the other side of the hedge while Mex and I were screwing in the space beside the window. They'd driven round to the flat, seen the curtains open and no lights on, and reckoned we'd gone somewhere else for the night. They must have come back today to watch the place for a while, maybe to question Mex. Matt walked right into it. In the rain, looking like me, where I was supposed to be. They must have seen him go in and got fed up waiting for him, for me, to come out again. Fuck it. They probably had a set of keys from Bigelow. Matt mightn't even have noticed them sneak in, didn't get a chance to open his mouth. Poor bastard. And I was in the bathroom admiring myself in the mirror. That was it. He was just an unfortunate, unlucky bastard. And I was a lucky bastard, wasn't I, lucky escapes again and again, one after the other? Shit, he was the lucky one, he's finished with it. They'll find out tomorrow or the next day that it wasn't me, and it will start all over again. It'll be worse than it ever was. I could feel myself starting to shake. McNabb was oblivious to what was going on, and kept on talking.

'. . . She was so freaked out that she didn't know where to go or what to do, so she got a taxi to my place. I didn't want her there, but what could I do? I tried to get her to calm down, to go home. But she wouldn't go. We talked for hours and drank too much booze. She said she needed to be with somebody. She told me that you two were finished, definitely, for once and for all. No going back. What could I do, Myles? I was drunk for Christ's sake.'

His voice had changed, but I didn't care any more.

'Give me the key to the car,' I said, and startled him out of his misery. 'I left my coat in the car, and I need to get some money from it. For more drink.'

'I can get it,' he said. I didn't know whether he meant the coat or the drink, but it didn't matter.

'Give me the key,' I repeated.

He looked at me curiously and handed me a small set of keys.

'Phone the Wife,' I said, and walked out.

It was starting to get dark outside, the kind of twilight half-dark that hovers around on summer nights, and it was still raining gently, a soft persistent drizzle. I looked at the yellow lamplight catching the tiny quicksilver dashes of colour, like a halo in the gloom, and I laughed at the thought of it. I walked calmly towards the shadowy bulk of the car, which glistened around the edges with a sickly sparkle of light. I imagined I could hear the river, lapping steadily against the cool green wetness of its banks.

I opened the car and slid into the driver's seat. I strapped myself in. I started up the engine and locked the doors. I opened the front windows a few inches. I slipped the car into reverse gear and looked behind me at the clear run to the shiny green railings and the river beyond. I knew that if I went into the Lagan in a locked car, I would never survive. I released the handbrake smoothly, quickly. Then I let it rip.

The car ploughed through the railings and crashed down over the bushes on the embankment and splashed into the river fast and hard. It creaked and started to sink. The cold water began to rush in along the floor and around the doors. It soon reached my knees. The car tilted a bit to one side and sank some more. I could see the level of the outside water rise up around the windows, and then start to pour in through the open gap on the passenger side. I braced myself for the cold chill as the river swirled and churned up around my waist, then my chest. I gasped for breath as the filthy grey water pushed upwards and bounced around my neck. I tilted my head back and took a last deep breath when I felt it splash up against my lips. I tasted the vile sweetness of it in my mouth. Then it stopped rising.

The car groaned and bubbled a bit and then tilted again, this time down at the back and up slightly at the front. Everything came to a frightening, sickening halt and I was left sitting there frozen into a limbo I could never have imagined. The water level stabilised and settled into a hard cold lapping movement around my chin, and everything outside the car went quiet and still. I didn't know what to do. I knew that I couldn't force myself under the water to drown. It couldn't be done.

I was still gasping for air, with the sudden shock of the cold water, and I pushed my head back instinctively to get more oxygen. I caught a glimpse of myself in the rear-view mirror. My face was at an angle, distorted, my mouth stretched open, and my eyes bulging and beaming in the strange oscillating light from the surface of the river. Another kind of shock, this time of recognition, ran through me. I looked like a half-strangled snake, choking on a forced reptilian scream. I started laughing. I couldn't stop myself from laughing.

I was still laughing when I heard voices and then shouts

and then energetic splashing sounds in front of the car. I couldn't see beyond the upwardly tilted bonnet, but I recognised McNabb's voice close by, cursing and shouting my name. I flipped off the lock on the car door and felt around for the catch on the safety belt. I was going to drag myself out and face the music. Then I hesitated. I sensed a shadow of someone struggling in the river just beside the window. I took a deep breath and closed my mouth and eyes, and then squirmed into the seat, wriggling downwards so that the water covered my head.

McNabb jerked the car door open, splashing and shouting, felt for my hair and pulled my head above water. He held me up and leaned behind me. He grabbed and pushed at me and called me all the assholes of the day until he got the seat belt undone, and then he hauled me out and dragged me to the bank.

I lay on the grassy slope coughing and rasping for all I was worth, holding my chest in pain, while he sat beside me gasping and spitting and looking at his car. Some people had gathered behind us, and I could hear a few of them joking about a lovely night for a swim. I couldn't blame them. I would have done the same. McNabb looked at me and called me a stupid bastard. I looked back at him and started to laugh again, a wet, croaky, painful laugh.

'What the fuck are you laughing at?' he asked in amazement.

'The dog's dead,' I spluttered, looking at the car. 'The dog's dead, good and dead, so the two fleas, the two of us, will have to walk home.'

He stared at me for a while. Then he remembered the joke. After fifteen years, he finally remembered the joke.

He burst out laughing, and the two of us sat and laughed and laughed, while the punters around us looked on in bewilderment.